"Am I disturbing you?"

Christa raised herself on an elbow and shaded her eyes. A man stood over her. She remembered him vividly from when she was a little girl. He was Matteo, her friend's brother.

"I suppose you're wondering what I'm doing here on the ground," she began lamely.

"Not at all. If you like to lie on the ground and laugh, that's your business."

He had just a hint of an accent, which added a certain something to his words.

She held out her hand, "I'm Christa Fraser, Pilar's friend.

"I know who you are."

"You remember me?"

Matteo's eyes took in the mussed blond ponytail and flushed cheeks of the woman before him. "I've often wondered how you turned out."

Dear Reader,

Welcome to Silhouette. Experience the magic of the wonderful world where two people fall in love. Meet heroines who will make you cheer for their happiness, and heroes (be they the boy next door or a handsome, mysterious stranger) who will win your heart. Silhouette Romances reflect the magic of love—sweeping you away with books that will make you laugh and cry, heartwarming, poignant stories that will move you time and time again.

In the next few months, we're publishing romances by many of your all-time favorites, such as Diana Palmer, Brittany Young, Emilie Richards and Arlene James. Your response to these authors and other authors of Silhouette Romances has served as a touchstone for us, and we're pleased to bring you more books with Silhouette's distinctive medley of charm, wit and—above all—*romance*.

I hope you enjoy this book and the many stories to come. Experience the magic!

Sincerely,

Tara Hughes
Senior Editor
Silhouette Books

BRITTANY YOUNG
All
or Nothing

Published by Silhouette Books New York
America's Publisher of Contemporary Romance

SILHOUETTE BOOKS
300 E. 42nd St., New York, N.Y. 10017

Copyright © 1987 by Brittany Young

ISBN: 0-373-08484-6

First Silhouette Books printing February 1987

America's Publisher of Contemporary Romance

Printed in the U.S.A.

Books by Brittany Young

Silhouette Romance

Arranged Marriage #165
A Separate Happiness #297
No Special Consideration #308
The Karas Cup #336
An Honorable Man #357
A Deeper Meaning #375
No Ordinary Man #388
To Catch a Thief #424
Gallagher's Lady #454
All or Nothing #484

BRITTANY YOUNG

lives and writes in Racine, Wisconsin. She has traveled to most of the countries that serve as the settings for her Romances and finds the research into the language, customs, history and literature of these countries among the most demanding and rewarding aspects of her writing.

Equator

Amazon River

● Brasilia

Rio de Janeiro
Sao Paolo ●

ATLANTIC
OCEAN

BRAZIL

Chapter One

Matteo Damiano stopped the Jeep on a hill overlooking his family's rambling home. The lush land that made up the Brazilian Damiano ranch stretched as far as the eye could see.

"It's beautiful, isn't it?"

Matteo looked at the man who sat next to him, then back at the view. "I remember coming up here with you when I was small and wondering how it was possible for one family to own so much land."

His father nodded. "But we did. And we do." He studied Matteo's profile. "I want you to come back here. I want you to join Damiano International."

"This is your life, not mine."

"But it could be yours."

"I like what I'm doing."

"You like what you're doing? Doctoring a bunch of people who can't even afford to pay you?"

Matteo said nothing. He and his father had been having this argument for years.

The older man climbed out of the Jeep and stood staring across the land, his hands on his hips. "You're impossible to reason with, Matteo."

"I'm told that I'm a lot like you."

The father turned to look at the son he loved, and a smile touched his mouth despite his frustration. "You are. That's why I want you here. You're the only one who can and will run things the way I would myself."

"You have Eduardo," Matteo said of his elder brother. "He'll do whatever you want. He always has."

His father nodded. "Eduardo is a good boy. And he tries very hard to do what's right. But he hasn't got your head for business."

"He's not a boy, Father. He's nearly thirty-five years old. You keep forgetting that."

"And you're thirty-three, and it's time you faced your responsibilities here."

"And it's time you realized that you and I have different ideas about what my responsibilities are. When I first started medical school, you thought it was a lark. When I graduated, you were sure I'd get over wanting to be a doctor. But it wasn't a lark, and I didn't get over it. Being a doctor isn't just what I do. It's what I am. I wish I could make you understand that."

His father shook his head sadly. "None of this would have happened if I hadn't sent your sister to live with Andrew Fraser while she attended that private school in Wisconsin all those years ago. I knew the moment you returned from a visit with Pilar and that family that you had changed, and it's Andrew's fault. If I'd known then what I know now..."

Matteo's lips twitched. "Dr. Fraser is one of your best friends and has been for decades. Admit it."

His father shrugged. "An aberration in taste that's lasted a long time."

"Is that why you hired his son, Mark, to run the ranch for you? An aberration?" Matteo asked dryly.

"I hired him because he knows what he's doing, and he's good at it."

"As I am good at my work."

"As are you," his father conceded with a sigh.

Matteo walked over to his father and put his hand on his shoulder. "You know that if you ever really needed me, all you'd ever have to do is say so and I'd be here. No hesitation. No questions asked."

"I know," he said quietly as he covered his son's hand with his own. "I know." Then he looked at his watch. "We should be getting back. Your mother's and my anniversary celebration starts soon. I'm glad you could make it back for this. It means a lot to your mother. And to me."

"I wouldn't have missed it. You take the Jeep back home. I think I'll walk."

"You'll be late."

"I'll walk fast. I need to think, and I do that better when I'm walking."

As Matteo watched his father drive off, he took a deep breath and slowly exhaled. Coming home was hard. He loved it here. He loved his family. But sometimes there was such guilt over the choices he'd made. He wouldn't change them, even if he could, but that didn't make it any easier to face his father.

Christa Fraser ran down the curving staircase of the sprawling Damiano villa and headed out the front door just as her brother opened it. Mark caught her arm and swung her around before she could race past him. "Where are you going in such a hurry?"

"Running."

"But you just got here an hour ago."

Christa kissed him on the cheek. "I know, and I can't thank you enough for inviting me." She took a deep breath and looked out at the ranch her brother managed for the Damiano family. "If you knew how cooped up I've been for the past three months, the only thing about this that would surprise you was that I held out for a whole hour."

He looked at Christa, standing there in her white shorts and pink tennis shirt, her long, very blond hair pulled back into a ponytail, a sweatband around her forehead, and tried to picture her as she must look when she interpreted meetings between staid and stuffy foreign diplomats. It was almost impossible.

Christa looked at him suspiciously. "Why are you studying me like that?"

"You've changed a lot since the last time I saw you."

"That was three years ago. I was fresh from college. I hope I've changed."

"You're all grown up."

Christa smiled at him. "You noticed!"

Mark tweaked her nose. "You go for your run. But don't be gone too long. The Damianos are having an anniversary party tonight, and we're invited."

"I'll be back in time."

"And stay on the main road, such as it is."

"I will." She kissed his cheek again and took off, waving over her shoulder at Mark. She ran across the wide expanse of green lawn, down the slight incline and past the arched, white stables to a road that was nothing more than tire tracks in the grass. All she could see were open pastures. After the past few months of being escorted by an armed guard everywhere she went in the Middle East, Christa felt as though she'd found a little bit of heaven. She kept her pace slow because it had been so long since she'd done any running.

A collie she'd never seen before barked and trotted beside her. But the dog got bored with the slow pace after a while and began racing ahead and stopping, his tail wagging madly, as he waited for her to catch up.

"Show off," Christa muttered under her breath, panting.

She could have sworn the animal smiled at her before running off again. But this time, to add insult to injury, the dog ran ahead and back, and then ran in circles around her. Christa, her blue eyes sparkling, started to laugh, until finally, out of breath, she stopped running altogether and dropped to her knees. The collie, showing no mercy, playfully nudged her onto her back and tried to lick her face. Christa laughed even harder.

"Am I interrupting something?"

Still smiling, Christa raised herself up on an elbow and shaded her eyes from the sun with one hand. A man stood over her. A very tall man with jet-black hair and brown eyes—nice brown eyes. A corner of his mouth lifted and the groove in his cheek deepened in reaction. Christa knew who he was. She remembered him vividly from when she was a little girl. His sister, Pilar, had been staying with her family. He was Matteo, the brother who would sometimes visit. Christa had half hoped to see him here. But she didn't want his first impression of her as a woman to be at a time when she was all flushed and sweaty.

"I suppose you're wondering what I'm doing here on the ground," she began lamely.

"Not at all." He took one of her hands in his and pulled her to her feet. "If you like to lie on the ground and laugh, that's your business."

He had just a hint of an accent, which added a certain something to his words.

She held out her hand. "I'm Christa Fraser, Mark's sister."

"And Pilar's friend. I know who you are."

"You remember me?"

Matteo's eyes took in the mussed blond ponytail and flushed cheeks of the woman before him as he held her hand in his. "I've often wondered how you turned out."

That was honest, and she was honest in return. "And I've often wanted to show you, but I always envisioned my big entrance in a ball gown with four-inch heels."

A slow smile curved his wonderful mouth. "I like you better this way."

That smile had started her heart pounding. "Good, because this is the real me."

"No one told me you were going to be here visiting your brother."

"It was kind of last minute. I just got here a little while ago."

Matteo looked up at the sky. "Well, I hate to put a damper on your run, but it's going to be dark out soon. You should be thinking about turning back."

Christa was having trouble taking her eyes from him. She began brushing the dirt from the back of her shorts, more for something to do with her hands than anything else. "I was just going to do that. Would you mind company?"

"Not yours." Again that smile curved his mouth and set her heart racing.

Christa smiled back, a surprisingly tentative smile for a woman who was rarely uncertain of herself, and Matteo found it enchanting, just as he found Christa enchanting.

He looped her arm through his as they started walking. "Do you still live in Wisconsin with your parents?" he asked.

"Not for quite a while. I'm in Washington now."

"D.C. or the state?"

"D.C."

"Do you have a job there?"

"I work for the State Department as an interpreter, so I'm based in Washington, but I don't spend much time there." The collie brushed against her leg, and she reached down to scratch his head as they walked.

Matteo studied her lovely profile, feeling strange. He'd known a lot of women in his life, but there was something about this one that was different. His reaction to her was different. "Are you married?" he asked suddenly.

Christa's engaging smile flashed. "I expected a little more subtlety from you."

"I don't have time for subtleties. I'm only going to be here for a few days."

It was strange to Christa, all these years later, to meet a man she'd had such a crush on as a child and to discover that those feelings had matured with age. She'd thought about him often over the years. She'd even asked Pilar about him whenever they'd spoken on the phone or exchanged letters.

She stopped walking and so did he. They turned to face each other. "I'm not married. And to be completely frank, I don't think I've ever been quite as pleased to be able to say that as I am at this moment."

His dark eyes rested on her face. He remembered her vividly as a child, and found himself wondering if he hadn't simply been passing time for all these years, waiting for her to grow into womanhood. And she had. With a vengeance. "Nor can I ever remember being quite so pleased to hear it. Be my guest at the party tonight."

"I'd like that very much. Thank you."

They stood there for a few more seconds just looking at each other. "We should be getting back."

"I know," Christa agreed, but neither of them moved.

The collie wiggled between the two of them and barked. Matteo's slow smile grew. "I imagine dogs would find this very boring."

"This one apparently does."

"We'll have to find him a girlfriend so he'll leave us alone."

They fell into step again. "What would you have done if I'd said I was married?" Christa asked curiously after a moment.

"Invited you, anyway."

"You cad."

"Dishonorable cad."

"That does add a certain something to it. Do you make a habit of dining with married women?"

"On the contrary. I avoid them diligently." He looked down at her. "You, however, would have been an exception."

"Why?"

He turned his head and looked at her with a half smile. "When a man meets the woman who's going to be the mother of his children, all is fair."

Normally Christa would have laughed at a remark like that, but Matteo didn't sound as though he were joking. There wasn't even a hint of a smile.

She had slowed down without realizing it, and now ran a few steps to catch up with him. From the corner of her eye, she discreetly studied Matteo's dark profile.

They walked the rest of the way in silence. A comfortable silence that lasted past the stables and up the hill to the sprawling villa. Matteo walked Christa through the arched doors and up the stairs to her room. She turned before opening the door and stood looking up at him. Matteo placed his finger under her chin so that she couldn't lower her face. His eyes moved from feature to feature, lingering and memorizing. Then he dropped his hand. "Don't take too long to change," he said softly.

Christa went into her room and then leaned her back against the closed door, placing her hand over her pounding heart.

A knock on her door nearly sent her through the ceiling.

"Christa?"

She opened it to find her brother standing there. "Hi. I thought I heard you. How was your run?"

"My run? Oh! You mean my *run*."

Mark looked at her curiously. "I guess I should have said that in the first place. How was it?"

"Fine. Just fine."

"Well, you'd better hurry. I saw from my window that some guests are already arriving."

"I will. Do you know where Pilar is? I asked a servant when I first got here, but he didn't seem to know."

"Shopping." Mark shook his head. "Shopping is her life, you know."

"Oh, it is not."

"I know, I know. It's just that when you live out here, you can't just hop in a car and go to a shopping mall. You hop on a helicopter and fly to São Paolo. And we both know how I feel about flying."

"The same way I do. You'd rather not, but sometimes you have no choice."

"What's your solution?" Mark asked.

"I just automatically assume that the plane I'm on is going to crash. It's amazing how calm that can make you."

"I don't think that would work for me," Mark said after a moment. "In fact, I don't think that would work for a lot of people."

"I suppose it does take a rather strange psyche. But you really should try it sometime. When the thing finally lands and you realize you've actually made it, it's like being handed a gift."

Mark smiled at her and hugged her. "I'd almost forgotten about you and your 'strange psyche.' It's good to have you here. I hope we have a chance to spend some time together."

Christa hugged him back. Mark wasn't the usual elder brother. He had never minded her tagging along with him when they were little, even though he was five years older. No one had to ask him to take care of her. He just did it naturally and easily. And if ever she was a pain, which she knew for a fact she frequently was, he never let her know it. Her brother was probably one of the nicest human beings to ever walk the face of the earth, and she loved him dearly.

Mark held her away from him and smiled. "You'd better get dressed for the party. I'll see you downstairs."

Christa quickly stripped, leaving a trail of clothes on her way to the bathroom. She showered and a few minutes later stood in front of her closet, wrapped in a towel, examining her sparse wardrobe. She had packed for only a few days, and there was really only one dress in the closet appropriate for tonight. It was periwinkle blue with a high neck and an open vee down her back. The waist was dropped and hugged her hips, and the skirt flared out just below her knees.

She finished drying herself off and slipped into the dress.

Then she brushed out her hair and studied it. It came to slightly below her shoulders in a thick, silky sheet, and she decided to just leave it alone. Her blue eyes had thick dark lashes that gave them a smudgy, soft appearance. Her skin was pale because she hadn't had much opportunity to be in the sun lately, but today's run had put some fresh color into her cheeks.

A gentle smile touched her mouth. The sun or Matteo Damiano?

There was a knock on her bedroom door, and she knew who it was. She looked in the mirror one last time, smoothed her already smooth dress and answered the door.

Matteo was leaning against the doorframe. His brown eyes took her in, starting at her feet and making their way slowly up her body. He stopped at her eyes, and a half smile touched his mouth. "Hello."

Her heart pounded. "Hello."

"You look beautiful."

So did he, in a tuxedo that was as black as his hair. "Thank you."

Then he held out his arm, and Christa placed her hand on it. Together they went down the winding staircase to the crowded rooms below. Doors that lined some areas of the villa had been thrown open to the gardens beyond. A string quartet played classical music. Uniformed men and women weaved among the guests, serving drinks and hors d'oeuvres.

Matteo propelled her gently toward his parents, who stood receiving people at the front door. "Mother," he said when they got there, "I know you've met Christa before, but not for a long time."

Christa extended her hand. "How do you do, *Senhora*?"

The older woman took Christa's hand in hers and kissed her, first on one cheek and then the other. "Please, call me Isabella. I'm sorry I didn't have a chance to see you when you first arrived, but things around here have been rather hectic today. How are your parents? It's been years since they were here."

"They're fine, living quietly while Father writes the book he's dreamed of finishing since he retired. They both wanted me to extend their good wishes to you."

As Christa turned to speak with Mr. Damiano, Matteo's mother studied her son as he watched Christa. The smile of a moment before faded into a more serious expression on his mother's face. Matteo had always been very discriminating about the women he spent time with; he seemed to have a preference for quality over quantity. But she had never seen her son look at a woman the way he was looking at Christa.

And when Christa turned her head and smiled at Matteo, the older woman saw a tenderness warm her son's eyes that surprised her. Matteo was a strong man, and cynical in many ways despite, or perhaps because of, his work. But not with this woman. She obviously touched something deep within Matteo.

When Christa had finished speaking with Mr. Damiano, Matteo kissed his mother's cheek, then put his arm around Christa's waist and walked her outside.

"Christa!"

She turned to find Pilar walking quickly across the lawn toward her. "Pilar!"

Christa hugged her friend, then held her away and studied her. "You look wonderful."

"So do you. It's been such a long time."

"I—"

Matteo reached around Christa and gently put his hand over her mouth. "If you think I'm going to spend the evening listening to your girlhood reminiscences, you're mistaken." He signaled to Christa's brother. "You take care of my sister, I'll take care of yours." And with that, he led Christa away. "Let's get something to eat."

He removed his hand from her mouth and wrapped a possessive arm around her waist. Her heart caught when he touched her, and she inhaled a little sharply. Matteo stopped and looked down at her. "What's wrong?"

"It's strange."

"What is?"

She looked into his eyes for a long, long time. "It seems as if the only part of my body I'm aware of when I'm with you is where you touch me."

Night had fallen, but the outdoor lights managed to provide a dim but warm glow. Matteo reached out and gently tucked her hair behind her ears. "We have some things to talk about."

She knew he was right.

His thumb rubbed against her mouth. "I knew the first time I saw you that you were someone special to me. But I didn't understand exactly what that meant until today."

"Eat now, get serious later," said a man in Portuguese as he walked by with a woman on his arm. He slapped Matteo on the back.

"That," Matteo explained, "is my elder brother, Eduardo, and his fiancée, Anna."

"I saw Anna earlier. She lives here, doesn't she?"

Matteo put his hand in the middle of Christa's back again as they walked toward the huge buffet. "That's right. She's lived here for the past seven years. Her father and mine used to be business partners. He arranged his estate plan so that if anything happened to him, all his holdings would revert to the Damiano family, and my father in turn promised that his oldest son would marry Anna."

Christa mulled that over as they walked. "What an odd arrangement."

"Not really. That kind of thing is very common here."

"But why didn't he just leave her the inheritance rather than making her marry someone else to get it? That hardly seems fair."

"Because he wanted to make sure she was taken care of, and he knew my father would see that it was done."

"That's wonderful of your father, but he isn't the one who has to marry her. Eduardo is."

"Eduardo expected to have an arranged marriage, and he's known about this thing with Anna for years."

"Is she in love with him?"

Matteo shrugged. "I really don't know. I haven't even spoken with her in anything more than a topical fashion for longer than I can remember."

Christa shook her head. "It just seems so cold-blooded."

"Perhaps if I tell you that my parents' marriage was arranged, that will help you understand what can often happen with these marriages. They fell in love with each other, and as you can see, they still are."

"I suppose. But I'm glad you're their number two son rather than number one."

Matteo smiled down at her as his hand rubbed against her back. "As am I."

When they got to the table, they each took a plate. There were some Portuguese foods and some native Indian dishes that looked and smelled delicious. Matteo helped himself, and when he noticed that Christa was taking next to nothing, he started putting food on her plate, as well.

"I can't eat all that," she protested.

He put another slice of beef on her plate. "But you can eat some of it."

Matteo guided Christa to a bench he had staked out under some trees. As they settled onto it and started eating, Christa glanced at Matteo's profile. He had grown quiet and thoughtful. "Is anything wrong?"

Brown eyes met blue, and softened. "Nothing that you need to worry about." He inclined his head toward her nearly untouched plate. "Eat."

Christa took a bite, but she couldn't get her thoughts away from Eduardo and Anna.

"Was a marriage ever arranged for you?"

Matteo laughed, a deep, rich sound that sent a delicious shiver through her. "What family in their right mind would want me married to one of their daughters? My existence is nomadic. I own little. I'm not what you'd call a very good prospect. That's something you should keep in mind as the evening progresses." He looked at her for a long moment. "Tell me, Christa Fraser, could you live with a man such as me?"

Christa knew what she was feeling—that she would find it difficult to live without a man like him—but she didn't know how to phrase it.

Matteo's eyes came to rest on her softly parted mouth. "Do you have any idea how beautiful I find you?"

Christa's gaze dropped, but Matteo reached out and raised her face to his. "I feel as though I've known you all my life."

She knew exactly what he meant. It was as though everything that had gone on in her life before now had been nothing more than a rehearsal for this moment. For this man.

His eyes roamed freely over her face, and then, as his eyes came to rest on hers, he shook his dark head. "There I was, out in the world, meeting women, but never the right one. Now I know why. I'd already met her. I just had to wait for her to grow up."

"And now that I have?" she asked quietly.

His thumb gently stroked her lips. "I don't know. My heart tells me that I should grab you and run, but my intellect points out the pitfalls in any future we might have."

"Such as?"

"Our lives are so different. I can't ask you to give up your work any more than you would ask me to give up mine. So where do we compromise?"

A woman in a maid's uniform walked by and took their plates. Night had fallen in earnest. Stars winked in the midnight sky as a chill settled in the air. Soft music still drifted across the lawn. Couples began dancing in the seductively lit courtyard. Matteo rose suddenly and held out his hand to Christa.

She looked at that strong, capable hand for a long moment before putting her own into it and getting to her feet. Matteo took off his jacket and draped it over her shoulders, then pulled her lightly into his arms and began swaying to the music. Their bodies didn't touch, but never had Christa been more aware of a man's nearness. Their eyes were locked as they moved. His hand at her waist pulled her lower body closer to his, until their hips and thighs touched and rubbed as they moved. And their gazes never wavered.

Suddenly Matteo stopped moving, even though the music still played. His eyes dropped to her mouth and slowly he lowered his lips to hers. He touched her lightly at first, and pulled away to look at her. He raised his hands to her face, gently running his fingers through her hair as he pushed it away from her face. Then he cupped the back of her head and lowered his mouth to hers again.

Christa felt a rush of passion so powerful she ached from its force. Her mouth parted beneath his, welcoming him, responding in a way she'd never dreamed herself capable. He was exquisitely gentle with her, rubbing his mouth lightly against hers, kissing the corners of her mouth, her bottom lip, her upper lip. Then he raised his head and gazed into her eyes before once again covering her mouth completely with his.

He began swaying slowly, rhythmically to the music as his mouth left hers once again. His hand gently pressed her head to his shoulder, stroking her hair, as his other arm wrapped around her, holding her close. She felt his mouth lightly brush her hair and then his cheek rest against it.

Christa sighed contentedly into his shoulder. This was so right there was no room for doubt.

"What are you thinking?" he asked.

She moved a little away from him and looked into his eyes. "That no mere job, no matter how much I love it, is going to keep me away from you."

Matteo stopped dancing and looked down at her. "Christa, I—"

A white-jacketed servant appeared out of nowhere and touched Matteo on the shoulder. "Excuse me," he apologized in Portuguese, "but you have a phone call."

Matteo's eyes were still on the woman in his arms. "I'll be right back."

"I'll be here."

He rested his mouth against her forehead, then walked toward the house.

Christa sat on the bench where they had eaten and pulled his jacket more closely around her to ward off the cold. As she rubbed her cheek against it, a soft smile touched her mouth. It smelled clean, like Matteo.

"Hello," a woman's voice said to Christa in English.

She looked up to find Anna standing beside her.

"May I sit with you?"

Christa moved over on the bench a little to make room. "Of course."

Anna had her dark hair pulled away from her face and into a low bun at the back of her neck. It was a severe but elegant style that suited her beautifully. She took some pins out of the bun and rearranged them, then looked at Christa and smiled. "You aren't what

I expected. Pilar talks of you often, but she never described what you looked like. I thought you would be taller, with darker hair.''

There was nothing Christa could say to that.

Anna studied her some more. "Things between you and Matteo look serious.''

Christa really didn't want to talk about Matteo with this woman. Not that she disliked her. She felt a little as though Anna were a victim. But she sensed something about her. It was as though Anna posed a threat to her somehow, which she knew was ridiculous, but it was a feeling Christa couldn't shake.

"It's a little too soon to tell.''

"I can tell. I've known him for years, and I've never seen him look at anyone the way he looks at you. You're very lucky. We both are, actually. Do you have any idea what power the Damiano name has? The doors it opens?''

"What are you talking about?''

Anna smiled a perfectly friendly smile at her. "There's no reason to pretend naïveté with me. You've been taking a dead aim at Matteo since the evening began.''

"And you think it's because of his last name.''

"You're human.''

"I see.''

"But I want to get one thing straight, because I think I like you, Christa, and I'd like for us to get along.''

Christa was finding this fascinating.

"Eduardo is the elder brother and I, as his wife, will become the mistress of this home and the official female family representative."

"I see." Christa nodded. "Then we won't have any conflicts. My—interests—lie in other directions."

Anna smiled again. "Good. I'll look forward to getting to know you better." She put one last pin in her hair and rose. "Well, I should be getting back to Eduardo. I just wanted to meet you and get to know you a little. I'm sure we'll be seeing each other later."

Christa's eyes reflected her amusement as she watched Anna walk away. She didn't quite know what to make of the woman. She hadn't been rude or threatening. She'd simply staked her claim. All in all, you had to respect someone like that. You might not like her motives, but at least you knew where she stood.

Christa turned her attention to the other people, scattered across the lawn. There were quite a few, perhaps a hundred or more. Some were dancing, some still eating, others standing in groups, talking and laughing. She saw Mark dancing with Pilar and smiled. They looked good together—and they were obviously used to dancing with each other. She wondered...

A warm hand came gently down on her shoulder. Christa rubbed her cheek against it. "You're back."

"I'm back," Matteo said softly, "and we need to talk."

She looked up at him, suddenly concerned. "You sound so serious."

"I am."

He took her hand in his and pulled her to her feet. "Let's go for a ride."

Christa assumed he meant in a car, until she saw that they were headed for the stables. Matteo wordlessly saddled a horse. He helped Christa to mount, then pulled himself onto the saddle behind her so that her back rested warmly against his chest. One strong arm went around her to hold the reins, the other rested low on her waist as he turned the horse out of the stables and headed across the ranch. They rode for about fifteen minutes, but it seemed like no time at all to Christa. He stopped the horse near a narrow stream that reflected the night sky and slid off, then put his hands at Christa's waist and helped her to the ground. For a long moment they just stood looking at each other. Then Matteo reached behind her and took a blanket from the horse and spread it on the ground beneath a tree. Matteo knelt on it and held out a hand to Christa. "Come here."

She did, going down on her knees in front of him. Matteo cupped her face in his hands and gazed into her eyes. "I want you to think about marrying me."

Christa's lips parted softly.

"I've never been an impulsive man, Christa. Everything I've ever done in my life has had a great deal of thought put into it. But with you, I know only what I feel. You complete the circle of my life. I knew it the moment I saw you today."

Christa smiled into his eyes and again his heart caught. "I did, too. So where do we go from here?"

"Not too far right now, unfortunately. I have to leave here early in the morning."

"Your work?"

He sighed. "My work. And before I finish, you'll be off doing yours." Matteo's thumbs stroked her cheeks. "I wish we had more than just tonight to talk about this. To be together."

"We'll meet again, as soon as we're both free."

"How will I get in touch with you?"

"Through the State Department. Sometimes the meetings I interpret are confidential. Even I don't know where I'm going until the last minute, and then I'm forbidden to tell anyone else. Security is difficult even under the best of circumstances these days."

"How long will you be gone?"

"At least four weeks."

His eyes rested tenderly on her face. "Do I need to worry about you?"

Christa smiled softly as she rested her mouth against his. "No. I'll be safe."

Matteo lay on the blanket, then pulled Christa next to him so that her cheek was on his shoulder. "Are you cold?" he asked as he nuzzled her hair.

"A little."

Matteo wrapped her in some of the blanket and then quietly held her. He should have been happy. How often was a gift like this simply handed to people? But he had a feeling. An uncomfortable foreboding that something was going to happen to keep them apart. Something he had no control over.

Matteo kissed the top of Christa's silky head and held her body even closer to his own. He couldn't lose her. Not now. He'd just found her.

Christa had never felt such utter contentment. Such peace. It was as though she'd come home after wandering aimlessly around for years. At last she was where she belonged.

Perhaps it was just as well that she couldn't see into the future, or she wouldn't have been able to enjoy even these few stolen moments with the man she loved.

Chapter Two

Christa leaned forward to stare out the helicopter as it approached the Damiano ranch, a three-week-old cable from Matteo clutched in her hand.

As she had so many times since leaving the Middle East for her trip here, she read the cable again. It said that Matteo's father and brother had been killed in an airplane crash. Three weeks ago! They'd been killed three weeks ago, and the State Department hadn't seen fit to pass the message on to her until yesterday because it didn't concern her immediate family.

Matteo had gone through all this alone.

The pilot made one pass over the villa, then set the helicopter down on a large, open stretch of lawn.

"Thank you!" she shouted over the noise of the whirring blade as she unfastened her seatbelt.

"What do you want me to do with your luggage?" he shouted back in Portuguese.

"Just set it on the lawn. I'll come back for it."

He inclined his head and reached into the back, while Christa jumped to the ground and ran toward the house.

"Chris!"

Her brother waved to her from the portico of the house and started walking toward her, catching her in his arms and hugging her. "Where have you been?"

"I just found out about Mr. Damiano and Eduardo yesterday. I got here as quickly as I could. How is everyone?"

Mark shook his head. "I don't think they really believe that it's happened. It's going to take a while for it to sink in."

"Is Matteo here?"

Her brother nodded. "I just saw him in the library."

She turned to go, but Mark stopped her.

"Chris, there's something you should know."

She turned and waited, alarmed at his tone. "Well?" she prodded when he said nothing.

Mark opened his mouth to speak, then closed it again. "Nothing. It can wait."

She kissed him on the cheek. "I want to see Matteo now. We'll talk later."

He gave her shoulders a gentle squeeze. "I have some work to do, but I'll try to finish up early."

"All right." She ran past him and into the house. The library was down a long hall. When she got to the closed library door, Christa stood quietly for a moment before knocking.

"Come."

She opened the door and stepped into the room. Matteo stood with his back to her, staring out a window. His blue-black hair was even longer than usual in back. "Matteo?" she said softly.

He stood still for a moment before turning and gazing at her. Then he wordlessly opened his arms and Christa ran into them.

"I'm so sorry."

His arms wrapped around her more tightly as he buried his face in her fragrant hair. Time stopped as they stood there.

After a time, Matteo moved Christa slightly away from him and gazed into her blue eyes. He raised a hand to gently caress her face as though getting to know her again. Christa turned her mouth into the palm of his hand and kissed it, then covered it with her own as she looked up at him. "I came as soon as I got your message."

He folded her back in his arms with a great sigh and rubbed his rough cheek against the top of her head. "I didn't know how much I needed to feel you near me until this moment."

She moved even closer.

Without Christa's knowing it, the door opened behind her and Anna Villa stood there, watching the scene. When Matteo raised his head and looked at the woman expressionlessly, she quietly backed out of the room and shut the door after her.

Matteo stared at the closed door, then once again buried his face in Christa's hair as a frown of pain creased his forehead. "We have to talk." He put his hands on her shoulders and held her away from him.

She remembered the last time he'd said that to her, and the joy she'd felt. But this time something was wrong, and it had to do with something other than his father and brother. "I'm listening."

Matteo dragged his fingers through his hair. "Things have changed."

She waited.

"I'll be staying in São Paolo now to head the business. There's no one else."

"And?" She prodded softly.

Matteo gazed into her eyes for a long moment, then turned away as though he couldn't bear to look at her. "I'm going to be marrying Anna Villa."

Christa was so astonished she couldn't speak.

"Eduardo is dead," Matteo explained, "but the obligation to Anna is still very much alive."

Christa felt as though she'd taken a direct blow to the stomach. "Matteo, you can't marry her."

"I have to."

"But you don't love her."

He turned back to Christa and looked at her with such tenderness that it nearly broke her heart. "You aren't listening, darling," he said softly. "Love has absolutely nothing to do with any of this. I'm head of the family now. Anna is my responsibility."

Christa just stood there, feeling helpless. "I don't understand this. It doesn't make sense. Doesn't Anna care that she's being passed from brother to brother like some—some piece of property? Where's her pride?"

"She's content with the new arrangement."

"Content?" Christa moved closer to Matteo, her heart in her eyes. "She's going to marry the man I love, and she's *content* with the arrangement?" Inside Christa was hysterical, but neither her voice nor her manner betrayed that. Only the man in the room with her knew what control she was exercising.

"Christa, please don't do this to yourself. It won't change anything."

She looked into his dark eyes. Eyes that told her how he felt. "How—" Her voice broke and she had to stop for a moment. "How can you marry Anna when you love me as much as you do?"

Matteo reached out a gentle hand and cupped her cheek. "I do love you, Christa. Nothing is going to change that. And I don't quite know what I'm going to do without you. But do without you I will. I know this is difficult for you to understand, but I have to do the honorable thing. First and foremost, I have to be able to live with myself. This is the only way."

"No," she whispered with a look of such pain that it nearly broke his heart.

Matteo pulled her gently into his arms and stroked her hair. "Oh, Christa," he said softly, "I wish there were something I could do to make this easier for you."

The hands she had laid flat against his chest suddenly clenched into fists, crumpling the material of his shirt as she buried her face in his shoulder. It was a moment before she regained control and was able to step away from him.

With a halfhearted smile, she looked apologetically at his wrinkled shirt and tried to smooth it out. "Oh, look at what I've done."

He caught her hand and brought it to his lips. "Don't worry about my damned shirt. Are you all right?"

She took her hand from his and impatiently wiped at some tears that had started to trail down her cheeks, annoyed at her weakness but unable to help it. "Just give me a minute."

She walked away from him to the window and stood with her back to him for the time it took to compose herself. "I'm sorry, Matteo," she finally managed, turning back. "After all you've had to deal with lately, I have no business putting you through this kind of emotional scene." Her throat constricted again, and once more she had to pause. "When I saw Mark a moment ago, I told him I'd be talking to him later, but I don't think I could face him right now."

"You just got here, Christa. You can't turn around and leave again."

"Sure, I can. It's not that long a flight back to Washington. I've done it before." She looked at him, but then had to look away. "As I was saying, I told Mark I'd see him later, but I really don't think I could stand it. Would you please..."

"I'll tell him you couldn't stay."

She nodded. "Thank you. I'd appreciate it."

There was a long silence between them.

"Do you know where your next assignment is going to be?" Matteo asked.

Christa shook her head, looking anywhere but at Matteo, wanting to run away but forcing her feet to remain still. "No." She cleared her throat again. Tears were so close, but she was determined not to let them fall. She tried to take a deep breath, but it caught halfway through.

Matteo wanted to pull her into his arms again, but didn't dare. He was afraid he'd never be able to let her go.

Christa forced herself to look at him. His pain was so obvious. Her head tilted a little to one side as her face filled with love. "Oh, Matteo," she said brokenly.

"I know," he said softly, reading her thoughts. "I know."

"I guess this is goodbye."

They stood staring at each other, not touching.

Then Christa took a deep breath, straightened her shoulders and, with all of the dignity in her, turned and left the room.

Matteo closed his eyes as he clenched his hands by his side. It was the only way he could keep from pulling her back to him.

It was the only way he could let her go.

He heard the front door of the villa close with finality behind her, and he lowered his head. It was over. She was gone.

When Christa finally made it outside, she ran away from the villa. The helicopter that had brought her was still there. The pilot was in deep conversation with someone who worked on the ranch. She ran across the lawn to him, holding her emotions in check as best she could. Out of breath, she stood before him. "I'd like you to take me back to São Paolo," she told him in Portuguese.

"Now?"

"Now, please."

"Sure."

He said goodbye to the man he'd been talking to while Christa climbed into the helicopter. A moment later they were airborne. Christa kept her eyes glued to the view, though she saw nothing. A few months ago her life had been so simple. She'd had a job she liked and a life with which she was content.

And then she met Matteo, and suddenly nothing was the same. She would never be the same. No matter how many years or how much distance she put between them, she would always love him. And wonder about him. And yearn for him.

She remembered hearing a long time ago that love hurt, but she hadn't realized until now exactly how devastating it could be.

Five months later, Christa stood outside her apartment door, doing a balancing act. Beside her on the floor was a large suitcase. Over one shoulder was a travel bag, over the other a huge purse. In one arm was a bag of groceries. A cellophane-wrapped pink rose was clutched between her teeth. She raised her knee to hold the groceries against the door while she rummaged through her purse, looking for keys.

A ringing came from within her apartment. She raised her head and grew still for a moment as she listened for it again. There it was, her telephone. She swore as best she could with a rose between her teeth and rummaged even more, through the used airline ticket, the passport, the paperback, until she felt the cool metal of her keys.

She pulled them out and fumbled with them, trying to select the one for her apartment. The groceries slipped a little, so she raised her knee higher as she inserted the key into the lock and turned the knob. But she couldn't keep her balance, and when the door suddenly swung open, she ended up hurtling through it. The bag split as the groceries crashed to the floor, sending boxes and cans everywhere. Torn between laughing and wanting to scream, Christa lay sprawled ignominiously on the floor, the rose still intact between her teeth.

The phone was still ringing, so she moved onto her side and reached up to the table for the receiver. "Hello?" she said as though nothing untoward had happened, rolling onto her back and staring at the ceiling.

"Christa?"

She raised up on her elbow, a sudden smile lighting her face at the sound of her brother's voice. "Mark! Where are you calling from? Are you in Washington?"

"No. I'm still at the ranch."

"Oh." She tried not to let him hear her disappointment. "It's a good connection. You sound as though you're in the next room. Is everything all right?"

"Couldn't be better. What are you doing for the next two weeks?"

"Resting and getting to know my apartment again. I'm happily between assignments for the first time in months. Why?"

"Because you're leaving on a jet bound for Brazil in exactly two hours."

Christa grew quiet. Brazil meant Matteo. Over the past five months she hadn't stopped loving him, but she'd learned to live with the fact that they'd never be together. She really didn't know if she could bear to see him again. "Mark, I just got home—literally. I don't want to leave again so soon."

"But you have to. I'm getting married, and I want you here with me. Neither Mom nor Dad can make it because of that book he's working on, so you have to come or I'll be the only Fraser.''

"Married?" she asked in amazement. That was the last thing she'd expected to hear.

"That's right. The wedding isn't for two weeks, but Pilar and I would both love it if you would come now. There's a lot of planning to do, and she could use the help."

Christa's thoughts hadn't caught up to her brother's. "Pilar? You're marrying Pilar Damiano?"

"That's right." Christa could hear him beaming with happiness right through the telephone line. "Please come share this time with us. Please, Christa. It would mean a lot to both of us. Especially to Pilar. She's had a lot of trouble adjusting to the death of her father and brother. She needs her best friend."

Christa felt herself weakening despite her own feelings. How could she say no when he asked like that? Surely she could forget herself long enough to share this wonderful moment with her brother and Pilar.

"Well?" he asked again.

Christa took a deep breath. Surely she could handle being around Matteo for a short time. She could handle it. "All right, Mark."

"Great! And thank you in advance for Pilar. So get your bags packed and head on out."

She couldn't help but smile at his enthusiasm. "You make me feel so wanted. And as I said, I'm coming, but not in two hours. I can't possibly pack and clear things up here in that amount of time. Besides, I need to make travel arrangements.''

"They've already been made. Damiano Industries has a plane in the U.S. even as we speak. It's making a special stop in Washington to pick you up, and then it's scheduled to leave the airport at six o'clock.''

"Is that what you were talking about? I thought you meant that there was a commercial flight out.'' Christa sat up straight and pushed her golden blond hair behind her ears, then looked at her watch and shook her head. "Mark, I'm really sorry, but I have too much to do. I haven't even had time to pay my bills or anything. I'm amazed my phone is still connected. Maybe in a few days—''

"Please, Chris? As I said, it's mostly Pilar I'm worried about. She needs you.''

Christa sighed with affectionate exasperation. "Have I ever told you how much I hate it when you beg?''

"Constantly.''

"Then why do you keep doing it?'' Christa asked.

"Because it works.''

"That's why I hate it. I promise that I'll do my best to make the plane.''

"That's my girl. Now get off the phone so you can get yourself packed.''

"Yes, sir.''

The line went dead. Christa held the receiver away from her ear for a moment before hanging up. She hugged her knees to her chest and stared sightlessly at the wall across from her. Well, she'd better start getting used to the idea of seeing Matteo again. How was she going to get through the next ten days?

With a sigh, she sat back on her heels to look at the mess she'd just made. Nothing would spoil if she were to leave it there. It was mostly canned goods. But she just couldn't do that. With a renewed sense of purpose, she gathered up an armload of groceries, lugged them into the kitchen and shoved them into the first cupboard she came to. Then she retrieved her suitcase from the hall, heaved it onto her bed and opened it to examine the contents. Considering that she'd been living out of it for nearly three months, its contents were pitifully few. And she was so tired of those clothes, she'd probably never wear them again.

She'd had everything washed and ironed before leaving Beirut, and now she put the things neatly away. Then she stood in front of her closet and stared at her wardrobe. How wonderful to have a choice again. But what to take? The weather in São Paolo would be in the seventies during the day, but the evenings were cool. She gazed longingly at all of the linens and cottons in her closet. They didn't travel very well, but in this instance she wouldn't be living out of a suitcase. With a smile, she pulled them out en masse and set them neatly into a hanging suitcase, then packed sweaters, jeans and warmer clothes into a regular suitcase. It was novel not to have to travel light.

Christa zipped one suitcase and snapped the lid down on the other. As she glanced at her watch, she saw she actually had a few minutes to spare, so she called her office and told them where she could be reached.

When she was ready to leave the apartment, she turned at the doorway and looked back in. What she wanted at that moment was to curl up with a good book on her very own couch in her very own apartment. She had missed having her own things around her. The apartment wasn't much, but it was her home. She liked it. She just never seemed to have any time to stay there. With a sigh, Christa closed the door and headed for the airport.

The cab ride was quick. Mark hadn't given her any information about where to meet the plane, but she assumed it would be in the corporate air terminal, and that's where she had the taxi drop her off. As she approached a desk to ask for information, a uniformed man stepped forward. "You are Miss Fraser?"

Christa looked at him in surprise. "Yes."

"Your brother described you to me." He took the suitcases from her hands. "I am Senhor Damiano's pilot. I'll take you to the plane."

"Thank you." She fell into step next to him as they walked through glass double doors and across the tarmac to the waiting jet. It was large, as private jets go, and in mint condition.

As Christa settled into the seat the pilot indicated she should use for takeoff, she gazed around the jet and liked what she saw. It was comfortable without being overly luxurious, and set up for a working person. A desk, a comfortable-looking couch and several swivel chairs with briefcase-size tables in front of them made up the main area.

When the pilot walked through the cabin after stowing her luggage, he indicated a small kitchen toward the front. "We have anything you might wish to eat or drink. Please feel free to help yourself."

"I will, thank you." She hadn't eaten for more than twenty-four hours, but she was too tired to be hungry.

A few minutes later the lights in the cabin went off, and the jet began its taxi down the runway. Christa fastened her seatbelt and stared through the window at the passing runway lights until they blurred into a straight white line. She felt the change from bumpy runway to smooth air as soon as the jet lifted off the ground. The jet made a steep ascent, and the landing gear thumped beneath her as it folded itself neatly into its compartment.

When the lights inside the cabin came back on, Christa relaxed her grip on the arms of her seat, and her white knuckles returned to a healthy flesh color. That was the only aspect of her behavior that indicated her fear of flying.

As she unfastened her seatbelt, Christa looked around the jet with a half smile. It was rather fun to have a jet all to herself. She got up to stretch and look around. The kitchen, although very small, was as well stocked as it would have been in a home. Another cabin served as a bedroom, again serviceable rather than luxurious. She also found a large bathroom, complete with shower and tub.

Christa eyed the tub wistfully, but settled for splashing her face with cool water and patting it dry with a hand towel. She opened the medicine chest in search of aspirin for a small headache that promised to turn into a real sledgehammer, found a bottle and swallowed two of the tablets with a glass of water.

As she was getting ready to leave, she noticed a bottle of men's cologne on the counter. Christa unscrewed the cap and sniffed the delicious, clean scent, then closed her eyes. It was Matteo's, and that cologne conjured his image so strongly in her mind that it was as though he were in the room with her.

And it hurt.

But, as if she were a glutton for punishment, Christa dabbed a little on the inside of her wrist and lightly sniffed. She walked back into the main cabin and settled onto the couch with the paperback that was still in her purse from the flight she had taken only a few hours before.

Her thoughts kept drifting, though, making it impossible to concentrate on the novel. She kept thinking about Matteo, wondering if he was married to Anna yet, wondering if he was finding any happiness in his life.

With a little shake of her head, Christa forced herself to pay attention to what she was reading. She made it through only a few pages before her eyelids started to droop. She had been traveling, one way or another, for more than twenty-four hours, and for the first time in her life, she was about to fall blissfully asleep on a plane. Setting the book aside, she stretched comfortably out on the couch, using one of the back cushions for a pillow. She barely had time to yawn before she was sound asleep.

Christa didn't feel the jet land half an hour later, or hear the pilot open the outer door and let down the stairs.

Matteo Damiano climbed aboard and started to say something to the pilot, but stopped when he saw Christa on the couch. A look of pain traced his features. "What's she doing here?" he asked the pilot in Portuguese.

The pilot looked at him curiously. "Your sister told me I was to pick her up."

When Matteo didn't say anything further, the pilot quietly went about his business.

Matteo crossed the cabin, set his briefcase on the desk and loosened his tie before going into the kitchen to get himself a drink. As he walked back to the desk, he stopped in front of the couch, one hand in his pocket, the other holding the drink, and looked down at Christa. She hadn't changed. She was every bit as beautiful as he'd remembered.

The jet started its taxi. Matteo still looked at her with tender eyes, cherishing her, before he reluctantly sat down to work.

At least, he tried to work. But he couldn't. His eyes kept returning to Christa. He hadn't expected to see her. He wasn't sure he was ready to see her again.

It hurt. He had made up his mind all those months ago as he stood in the library, watching her suffer, that it would be best for both of them if they cut each other out of their lives completely. But now he didn't know which was worse, not seeing her at all, or looking at her and knowing they couldn't be together.

Christa kept moving restlessly in her sleep. Every time she moved, he looked up from his work. Suddenly, she shot up into a sitting position, gasping for breath, her eyes wide open but unseeing. Matteo was in front of her within seconds, his strong hands holding her shoulders with firm reassurance. "Christa? Christa?"

Christa's eyes slowly focused on Matteo's face, less than a foot away from her own, and her confusion faded. She wasn't in Beirut at all. She was here, safe with Matteo.

He reached out a gentle hand and tucked her mussed hair behind her ear. "Are you all right?"

She was breathing hard, as though she'd been running. "I am now."

Matteo straightened away from her and went into the kitchen. Christa's eyes, a hunger in their depths, followed him.

He emerged a moment later with a snifter of brandy and folded her lightly trembling fingers around it. "This should help a little," he said quietly.

Christa cradled it gratefully as Matteo lowered himself into a chair across from her.

"I wasn't expecting you to be on this plane. Mark didn't say anything about that when he called."

"No one told me, either."

"It seems strange, sitting here with you like this."

He touched the bottom of the snifter. "Take a sip."

She did, her eyes never leaving him. It was as though she were afraid he'd disappear if he left her sight.

Matteo gently traced a finger along the shadows under her eyes. "You look tired, Christa."

She was so aware of his touch that she hardly heard his words. "I am."

"I've asked Mark about you, but he never seems to know much."

"I wasn't able to contact him for the past three months."

"One of those sensitive interpreting jobs?"

She nodded.

"I'm glad you're safe. I've wondered about you. Worried about you."

"There's no need."

A corner of Matteo's mouth lifted as though to say that there was every need. His eyes searched every inch of her face, getting to know her all over again. "I've missed you."

Christa had to swallow hard. "I've missed you, too. Are you . . . are you and Anna married yet?"

"No. I'm surprised Mark didn't tell you that."

"I didn't ask."

Matteo looked at her with dark eyes. "You don't know, do you?"

"Know what?"

"The wedding Mark invited you to help with is a double wedding. Your brother and Pilar, and Anna and I."

Christa lowered her head. "He didn't say a word about that," she said quietly. "Not a word. Only that he and Pilar needed me there."

"I'm sorry, Christa."

"It's not your fault." She thought for a moment. "Can you have the pilot turn the plane around and take me back?"

"No. I have a meeting when we land tomorrow that I can't miss. He can take you back after that."

"Do you want me to go?"

Matteo caressed her with his gaze. "I want you to do whatever is best for you. The last thing I want to do is to cause you any more pain."

Christa's heart was in her eyes. These past months without him had been almost unbearable. Not a day or night passed that he wasn't in her thoughts.

"Don't look at me like that, Christa."

"I can't help it."

"You'll have to help it." He got to his feet. "We won't be in Brazil for hours. You might as well try to get some rest."

She lowered her eyes and nodded.

"Finish the brandy first."

While she obediently drank what was left in the snifter, he pulled out a blanket from a closet, then took the empty snifter from her fingers and set it on a small table next to the couch. He put his hand on her shoulder and softly pressed her back onto the couch. "It's a little chilly in here," he explained as he draped the blanket over her. "You'll be glad for this later."

"Thank you."

Matteo straightened and gazed down at her. "Good night," he said quietly, then went back to his desk.

All of the cabin lights were off except the lamp fastened to Matteo's desk. Christa found herself watching him. His oversize white shirt had the sleeves rolled halfway up his powerful, tanned forearms, exposing a black leather-banded watch. The top button of his shirt was undone and his tie loosened. He was very well put together, but there was nothing studied about it.

Suddenly Matteo snapped off the lamp on his desk, leaned back in his chair and swiveled slightly toward the window to stare out into the blackness. Christa strained her eyes against the darkness in the cabin to see him, but gave up after a few minutes, took a deep breath and slowly exhaled.

Even as she drifted into sleep, she sensed Matteo's presence, and she felt safe and warm. The yearning was still there. But at the moment, all that mattered was that he was with her.

Chapter Three

When Christa awoke, everything was still. There was no hum from the jet engines, no movement. She slowly opened her eyes and looked around. Light streamed in one of the plane's windows. She was still on the couch.

The same pilot she had met at the airport walked in from the cockpit and smiled when he saw that she was awake. "Good morning," he said in English.

She returned the smile as she sat up. "Good morning. Where's Mr. Damiano?"

"He left the jet a few hours ago when we arrived in São Paolo. You were sleeping so peacefully he decided to leave you alone. I'm to take you back to Washington as soon as the jet has been checked and refueled. If you'd like to freshen up, the bathroom is toward the back and your luggage is stored in a small room just beyond here.''

''Thank you.''

''Hello!'' came a greeting from behind the pilot.

Christa looked past the man to find Pilar standing in the door of the plane, smiling at her.

As happy as she was to see her friend, Christa was more annoyed. ''Hi, Pilar.''

''Uh-oh.'' She walked farther into the plane. ''It sounds like I'm in trouble.''

''When Mark called me, he didn't say anything about a double wedding.''

Pilar grew serious. ''I know. I asked him not to because I was afraid you wouldn't come.''

''I wouldn't have.''

''See? I was right.''

''You can't expect me to come to Matteo's wedding.''

''I didn't want you to come to his wedding. I wanted you to come to mine.''

''You'll forgive me if I don't see the distinction.''

''Christa, I can't do this without you. I need you.''

''You have Mark.''

''And I love him very much, but I need you. We've been best friends since elementary school. You can't bail out on me now. I won't let you.''

Christa looked out the window and then at her friend. ''I'm going back to Washington today.''

Pilar didn't say anything, but her great, dark eyes filled with tears.

Christa clicked her tongue. "Oh, Pilar, don't do that. Please. It's not going to help anything."

"I can't marry Mark. That's all there is to it. Not yet, anyway."

"What are you talking about?"

"There's so much to do. A house to get ready. And I keep thinking about my father and Eduardo." She shook her head. "I miss them so much."

Christa walked over to her friend and hugged her. "I know. I'm sorry."

"And now you're deserting me," she said.

Christa thought about Mark's voice when he'd called to tell her about the wedding and how happy he sounded. "All right. I'll stay, Pilar. For a while, at least."

"Thank you. It means a lot to me." She plucked a tissue from a box on a table and dabbed at her eyes. "And now I'm going to take you out to lunch. There's a car waiting for us on the tarmac."

Christa looked down at her rumpled self. "I have to get cleaned up."

"How long do you think that'll take?"

"Half an hour."

Pilar sat down with a magazine. "I'll wait here."

With a little shake of her head at the way her friend's moods could change, Christa found her luggage and pulled out her makeup and something to wear. After running the water into the bath and sinking into it, Christa began to wish she'd told her an hour. What a luxury. But after a few minutes, being the disgustingly responsible person she was at times, she dried herself off and slipped into the full pale pink dress and white linen jacket she'd packed, pushing the sleeves slightly up her forearms and lifting the collar in the back. She brushed her hair with long strokes until it curved just below the collar and then fluffed up the bangs a little. She put on some makeup, but not much. Just enough to give her cheeks and mouth some color.

"Christa?"

She zipped her makeup bag shut and stepped out of the bathroom to find Pilar standing just inside the cabin door.

"Are you ready?"

"Yes. What should I do with my luggage?"

"The pilot will see that it's sent on to the house."

They left the plane, and a chauffeur stood at an open car door, waiting for them. Christa looked back at Pilar as she climbed in. "Such service."

When they were both in, the driver took off, crossing the tarmac and going through an open gate in a chain-link fence. They were headed toward downtown São Paolo. The size of this city never ceased to amaze Christa. It was so unexpected. It was like being in the middle of nowhere and suddenly stumbling upon a teeming metropolis of towering buildings, congested traffic and wide crowded sidewalks. Cars, taxis and buses choked the streets, slowing traffic to a crawl. Christa almost felt as though she were in New York rather than Brazil, but the sight of an occasional banana tree or a woman food vendor in her bright traditional clothes helped put things in perspective.

After forty minutes of fighting traffic, the driver double parked in front of a modern skyscraper. Christa stared up at the shiny aluminum letters that spelled out DAMIANO INTERNATIONAL, then looked at Pilar. "Why are we here?"

"We'll just be a minute. Matteo is expecting us."

"Pilar—"

Pilar turned to her friend. "Look, Christa," she said gently, "you're going to be at the ranch for at least two weeks. Matteo lives there. You're going to be seeing a lot of each other, so you'd better get used to it. Now come on."

Christa followed Pilar out of the limo and went into the building through the electric sliding doors. Two guards sat at a circular desk in the middle of the lobby with computer terminals and numerous closed circuit televisions surrounding them. Pilar walked over to one of them and waited until he finished speaking on the telephone. "¿Sí?"

"My name is Pilar Damiano and I'm here to see my brother, Matteo."

He pressed some keys on his computer. "He's expecting you." He handed her a badge with a number on it and then looked at Christa.

"Oh," Pilar explained, "she's with me."

"Your name?" he asked Christa in Portuguese.

"Christa Fraser."

He made a note of it and clipped a badge on her jacket.

There were several elevators open and waiting, but Pilar wanted one in particular. "This one goes to a higher floor," she explained, and pulled Christa on after her as soon as it arrived.

A few seconds later it stopped, and the doors opened. Christa stepped out directly into the middle of some very busy executive offices. Pilar went straight to the receptionist a few feet away. "I'm here to see Matteo Damiano."

"Go to the end of the hall, turn left, and his offices are straight ahead from there."

"Thank you."

"Don't you know your way around?" Christa asked.

"I haven't been here since I was a child. It's completely changed."

They followed the receptionist's directions and found themselves standing in front of yet another desk, but there was no one behind this one, so they waited.

A middle-aged woman, her dark hair graying slightly at the temples, came from out of nowhere and smiled at them. "Miss Damiano and—"

"Christa Fraser," Pilar filled in for her.

"Miss Fraser. This way, please."

They were led into an enormous office. Matteo sat behind his desk, talking on the phone, but looked up when the women entered. His eyes went straight to

Christa, and he stopped speaking in the middle of a sentence. His dark eyes hardened as he waved them into chairs across from him, and Christa's heart constricted. His secretary left, closing the door behind her, but Christa was barely aware of that. Matteo's presence filled the room for her to the exclusion of anyone or anything else.

He rose from behind his desk, still speaking into the phone, and walked to the windows to look out over the city. He was speaking in rapid Portuguese that Christa understood very well, but she didn't hear a word he said. Rather, she listened to the way he said it. His voice was deep and quiet and slightly husky.

Her eyes drank in the sight of him, roaming shamelessly over his broad shoulders and down his long, leanly muscled body.

When he finished talking, he turned back toward Christa and hung up. Then he half leaned, half sat on his desk and gazed at her for a long moment before speaking. "Good morning."

"Good morning."

"I wasn't expecting to see you today."

"I wasn't expecting to be here." Christa looked meaningfully at Pilar and Matteo followed her gaze.

"What's going on?" he asked his sister.

"I talked Christa into staying."

"Why? She obviously doesn't want to be here."

"I need her, and she agreed to stay. And you and I have a lunch date, but I couldn't very well leave Christa by herself while you and I went out."

"Look," Christa interrupted, "I really hate being talked over as though I weren't in the room. Pilar invited me for lunch without bothering to tell me she had a previous engagement with you. If I'd known, I would have declined." Then she looked at Pilar. "You and Mark seem to be having a problem with telling me things lately."

Pilar lowered her eyes.

Christa got to her feet. "I'll go shopping or something until the two of you get back."

"Christa."

She turned back from the door at the sound of Matteo's voice. "What?"

"Come to lunch with us."

"I really don't—"

"Come on. Surely we can be together for one lunch."

Pilar looked hopefully at her.

Christa met his gaze for as long as she could, then dropped her eyes. "All right."

Pilar looked at her watch and suddenly leaped to her feet. "Excuse me, you two, but I have to make a phone call." She left the room and Christa stood there, feeling a little lost.

Matteo's eyes softened as he looked at her. "Did you get some sleep this morning?"

She nodded.

"The shadows under your eyes are lighter."

She looked at him for a moment. "I'm really sorry about this, Matteo."

"It's not your fault. I think your brother and my sister are unfortunately under the mistaken impression that they can bring us back together."

Christa's eyes met his. "You're handling this very well."

"Am I?" Matteo wanted to take her into his arms so badly he ached.

"You know, when I get to the ranch, it's going to be difficult for us to avoid each other."

"Very."

She lowered her eyes for a moment, then forced herself to look directly at him. "It hurts being near you."

"Almost as much as it hurts to be apart," he said softly.

"Almost."

Matteo walked to her, then reached out and cupped her chin in his hand. "Just for today, let's enjoy each other. Tonight, when we go back to the ranch, we'll start our separate lives all over again."

"All right," she agreed. "Just for today."

Pilar walked back in at that moment, looked at the two of them standing so close and tried desperately not to smile. "I'm afraid I have to run over to the dressmaker's for a quick fitting. I'll have to meet you at the restaurant."

Matteo looked at his sister and shook his head. "You and I are going to have a little talk later." He pressed an intercom button and spoke to his secretary in Portuguese, then put his hand under Christa's elbow and escorted her out a back door to yet another elevator just outside his office. They stepped inside, and Matteo inserted a key. The doors closed, and the elevator went straight to the lobby. Then he removed his key and walked her out of the building. "I hope you like Indian food," he told her as they sidestepped the people walking toward them.

"East Indian or South American Indian?"

"East."

"I love it."

They walked about two blocks to a small restaurant that had no sign, only a menu on a reading stand under a canopy. The owner greeted them at the door and seated them at a secluded table in a darkened corner. A moment later, a waiter approached, and Matteo looked at Christa. "What would you like to drink?"

She thought for a moment as she unfolded her napkin and laid it across her lap. "Sparkling mineral water with lemon."

"Two."

When the waiter had gone, Christa looked at Matteo and smiled softly. "It was rather strange seeing you in the office. You looked surprisingly at home."

"It's a new challenge."

"Do you miss your other life?"

"Of course. But I've found other ways of seeing that what I was doing before still gets done."

"How?"

"By setting up free clinics. It doesn't matter who does the doctoring as long as it gets done." His dark eyes softened as he looked across the small table at Christa. "What I really want to talk about is you. What have you been doing?"

"Working mostly."

"Where?"

"Beirut."

"Beirut? You have no business being in a place like that."

Christa grinned suddenly. "It's a dirty job, but somebody has to do it."

Matteo's smile flashed, but then he grew serious. "You shouldn't be making light of it. If you were my woman—" Matteo suddenly stopped when he realized what he'd said, then started again in a soft voice. "If you were my woman, I wouldn't let you go."

She thrilled to his words and the possessive way he looked at her when he spoke them, but she forced herself to keep things light. "If I were your woman," she countered, "you wouldn't have a choice."

"Ah, you talk back."

"In five languages."

The two smiled at each other, and Christa relaxed a little. She didn't have to be on guard against Matteo. He would never do anything to dishonor either her or Anna.

"What are you thinking?" Matteo asked.

The waiter brought their mineral waters and then Matteo, with Christa's silent permission, ordered lunch for both of them.

"Now," he said when he finished, "I had asked what you were thinking."

"I know. I was wondering what to tell you."

"What's wrong with the truth?"

"My truth or yours?"

"Ours."

A smile touched her mouth. "I was thinking that you're an honorable man. I like that about you." She paused. "I love that about you."

"I'm not as honorable as you think, Christa." His eyes gazed into hers.

"Meaning?"

"Meaning that what I really want to do right now is take you to my apartment and make love to you for the rest of the day."

"What about Pilar?"

"You know as well as I do that she isn't going to show up. This is her way of throwing us together."

Blue eyes met brown. "Then why didn't you take me to your apartment?"

"Because with you, I either have to have all of you or nothing. I can't have you once and then never again. I can't make love to you and marry someone else." He paused. "And I have to marry someone else."

Christa lowered her eyes. "I think I was hoping that Anna would have changed her mind."

"She won't. It's not something you should count on."

The waiter served their food and made a polite exit. Christa picked up her fork and halfheartedly pushed things around, not really realizing what she was doing.

An argument between a man and a woman erupted at another table, and Christa turned her head to see what was going on. Matteo's eyes rested on Christa's profile. She was so lovely. Not just physically, though he found even that heart stopping. But she was a good person, beautiful from the inside out. And he had missed her.

"Christa?"

She turned back to him.

"Your food."

"Oh." She smiled at him. "Sorry." She inhaled the deliciously scented steam rising from the food before taking a bite and sighing. "I had no idea I was this hungry."

"When was the last time you ate?"

"A day or two ago. I don't usually have much of an appetite when I travel."

Matteo watched her eat for a few minutes. She may have been hungry, but her bites were as delicate as she was.

They finished their meal in a companionable but aware silence, and then the waiter came to clear away the dishes. Matteo looked at his watch and asked for the check. "As much as I've enjoyed this lunch—" his eyes touched hers "—and your company, I have to get back to my office for an appointment."

"What should I do?"

"Come back with me. Pilar will show up with some lame excuse about the fitting taking longer than she expected. Then the two of you are going to have to wait until I finish with my appointment before we fly to the ranch."

"How long will that be?"

"An hour. Possibly less. You might want to take a walk around the city rather than just sitting around."

"I think I will. Thank you."

A car suddenly backfired outside the restaurant. Christa jumped so violently that she sent her water glass crashing to the floor.

Matteo frowned as he reached across the table and caught her hand in his. "What is it?"

"This is really embarrassing. I'm sorry."

"Why did you jump like that?"

Christa smiled sheepishly. "I thought it was a gunshot."

But Matteo didn't return her smile, and as they sat there, Christa went from embarrassment to awareness of the strong, warm hand holding her own.

Matteo's hand tightened on hers for a moment, then he released it. "Let's go." He tossed some money on the table and rose, then held Christa's chair out for her and put his hand in the middle of her back to guide her out of the restaurant.

On the walk back to his building, Christa tried to push the fact of Matteo's nearness from her mind, but she couldn't, even with all of the colorful distractions São Paolo offered.

The sidewalks, even though they were a boulevard wide, were crowded, and it was impossible to walk without being jostled. Matteo's hand moved from her back to her waist and pulled her closer to his side in a protective gesture.

When they got to his building, Matteo signaled to one of the guards behind the desk and then looked down at Christa. "I'll try to break away by three. We can meet in the lobby and leave for the ranch from here."

"All right."

The security guard walked over to them and Matteo spoke to him in Portuguese as Christa listened in surprise. "I don't need an escort," she protested quietly.

Matteo looked down at her for a long moment. "Perhaps not, but humor me, Christa. I'll feel better if I know you're not alone."

Christa's curious gaze followed him across the lobby.

"Miss Fraser?"

She turned toward the security guard.

"Are you ready?"

She took a deep breath and slowly exhaled. "No, I don't think I am," she answered, but she wasn't talking about exploring São Paolo.

* * *

Christa and the security guard arrived in the lobby at almost exactly the same time as Matteo. Her heartbeat accelerated as she watched him walk toward her.

"So, what did you think of São Paolo?" he asked as he came to a stop in front of her.

"It's a city. Big, crowded and impersonal."

"And you prefer the country?"

"Every time."

"There you two are!" Pilar came rushing in. "I went to the restaurant, but you'd already gone."

"Did the fitting take longer than you'd expected?" Christa asked innocently as Matteo flashed her a quick smile.

"Much longer. And then when I couldn't find you, I came here and was told that you'd gone out and that Matteo was in a meeting, so I did a little last-minute shopping. Are we going home now?"

Matteo looked at Pilar and shook his head. "How did you say all that without taking a breath?"

Pilar grinned at him.

"Let's go." Matteo put his hand in the middle of Christa's back and headed for the elevators. Pilar followed close behind.

The elevator took them to the roof, where a helicopter waited. Matteo helped Pilar into the back seat and Christa into the front and then climbed in behind the controls. He put on a set of headphones and began talking into a small microphone in front of his mouth as he pushed buttons and flipped switches that got the blade slowly whirring. He spoke again, in

Portuguese, and asked for permission to take off. As soon as it came, he got the blade whirling at full speed and lifted away from the rooftop to swoop over the city and its traffic jams.

Christa was watching out the window at the sights that were beginning to be familiar to her, but she wasn't really seeing them. Her awareness of the man seated next to her was almost overwhelming. Would that ever end?

Pilar kept up a steady stream of chatter during the ride, but she had to yell over the noise. When Matteo finally landed the helicopter on the lawn, Christa was surprised. It hadn't seemed anywhere near an hour.

Matteo climbed out and walked around to the passenger side to open the door. He put his hands at Christa's waist and lifted her to the ground. He seemed oblivious to the physical contact between them, but she knew he wasn't.

"Christa!"

Mark strode toward her from the direction of the stables. With a smile that came from her heart, Christa ran straight into his arms. Mark hugged her tightly. "It's good to see you."

She moved slightly away from him and looked at his happy face. "It's good to see you, too. You look wonderful."

He frowned a little as he touched her cheek. "And you look pale."

"Nothing that a little fresh air won't take care of."

Mark wrapped his arm around her shoulders and walked her toward Matteo. "Thanks for bringing her."

Matteo looked at him in cool silence. "Yes. We'll talk about that later."

Mark cleared his throat nervously. "Is Pilar with you?"

"Coming!" her voice called from inside the helicopter. "I can't find my other shoe." There was a pause. "There it is."

Mark lifted Pilar out, and they had a little meaningful eye contact while Matteo looked at his watch. "I have a phone call to make. Your luggage arrived earlier, Christa, and is already in your room. I'll see you later."

"And I have to run, too." Pilar kissed Mark and then Christa. "See you at dinner."

Christa looked at Mark expectantly. "Well, now that you've gotten me here, are you going to desert me, too?"

Mark grinned at her. "I almost hate to tell you this, but I only have a few minutes."

"What a surprise."

He pulled her arm through his and held it close to his side. "Hey, a few minutes is better than nothing. Come on."

They walked in the same direction as Matteo, toward the villa. It was still early afternoon, but cool. As they were about to go up the steps and into the house, Christa put her hand on her brother's arm. "Could we go around to the back and sit by the gardens for a while. I don't want to go inside just yet.''

"Sure." They walked around the villa and found two cushioned chairs beneath a shady tree about ten yards from the house and sat down. Christa looked at her brother, who sat across from her, with a long and steady gaze.

"You've done a few things lately that I don't understand, Mark. Maybe you can clear them up for me."

He waited, knowing full well what was coming.

"Why didn't you tell me on the phone that Matteo and Anna are getting married at the same time as you and Pilar?"

"I'm sorry about that, Chris. It bothered me. But Pilar and I discussed it. We knew you wouldn't come if we told you, so we thought it would be best simply to keep quiet about it. Are you angry with us?"

"Am I angry?" she asked in amazement. "I can't believe how insensitive you are. It's not like you, Mark. No matter how much I want to see you and Pilar get married, I can't come to the wedding. You can't expect me to."

"You're right. I'm sorry," he apologized, but there was a glint in his eye that said he wasn't really sorry at all.

"And then to have Matteo on the same plane with me..."

"Tell me you didn't enjoy seeing him again and being able to spend time together."

"I can't tell you that," she said quietly, "but I wish you hadn't. It hurts."

Mark reached across the short distance separating them and took her hand in his. "You know that I love you, Chris."

"I know."

"And I would never do anything to deliberately hurt you."

"I used to know that, too."

"Well, you should still know it. But there are times when you just have to put your trust in your older brother."

"Times such as these?"

"Times exactly like these."

"You make it difficult. I don't even know what to believe. Pilar told me she was having a hard time because of all that's happened here, but now I don't know whether she really means it or if it's another little trick the two of you dreamed up to push Matteo and me together."

"She means it," Mark said quietly. "It's been rough around here. She called off the wedding once because she didn't think she could go through with it so soon after...you know. But her mother and I talked her into going ahead with it. We'll stop what we've been doing, but don't leave."

Mark rose and kissed her cheek. "And in case I didn't tell you on the phone, I think you're wonderful to come at all. So does Pilar. She knows it isn't easy."

"What exactly does she want me to do?"

"Women's stuff."

Christa's mouth twitched. "Women's stuff?"

"Sure. You know what I mean."

"Oh, I know what you mean, all right. But I dare you to repeat that to Pilar."

Mark grinned at her. "You're right. She'd nail me." There was a pause. "So," he said a little too casually, "what'll it be? Will you stay?"

"I'll consider it."

"You'll consider it?"

Christa nodded. "I don't think I can put it any more clearly for you."

He stood there looking at her.

"Didn't you say you had work to do?"

His eyes widened. "I almost forgot. You just sit here and—"

"Consider it," she finished for him.

"Right. We'll talk later."

"I'm sure we will," she said dryly.

Chapter Four

Her smile faded after her brother left. The reality was that she'd be staying in the same house as Matteo. She'd be seeing him all of the time—and Anna.

There was something, after all, to be said for staying for the wedding. If she could see things through to their conclusion—if she could actually see Matteo married to Anna—then it would put a period to whatever dreams she might have. It would be over, in living color, and she could start her life again. Without Matteo.

Christa rose with a sigh and went into the villa. The first people she saw were Anna and Matteo, standing in the foyer, quietly talking. Christa paused, hoping they would go away, then realized how ridiculous she was being and decided to brave it out. She took a deep breath and approached them. "Excuse me."

They both looked at her. "I don't know which room I've been put in."

It was Matteo who answered her. "The same one you had last time."

"Thank you. I think I'll change and go for a walk." Then she looked at Anna and tried to smile, but couldn't quite pull it off. "Hello, Anna."

Anna inclined her dark head. "Christa."

Christa moved past both of them. When she got to her room, she closed the door behind her and leaned her back against it. The first encounter was over with, and she'd survived. She'd survive the next one, too.

Feeling a little better about things, Christa changed into some jeans and an oversize sweater that fell halfway down her thighs. She fastened the Velcro straps of her running shoes, then left the villa and walked to the stables. When she got there, she narrowed her eyes a little to adjust to the interior dimness.

"Hello," someone said in Portuguese.

Christa narrowed her eyes even more and saw a wizened little man about fifty feet away, brushing down a horse. "Hello," she answered, also in Portuguese. "Would it be all right if I borrowed a horse?"

He apparently knew who she was, because his nut-brown face folded into a hundred smiling wrinkles. "Senhor Mark's sister can borrow any one she wishes."

Christa smiled back at him. "It's nice to have friends in high places. If you have a horse who's just a nice basic, everyday kind of horse without dreams of someday winning that big race, that's the one for me."

Again he smiled. "I have one who's perfect." He walked toward her and stopped at a stall a few feet from where she was standing. Christa moved to stand next to him and looked through the gate at a moderately sized white mare with great dark eyes. Christa reached into the stall and stroked the silky nose.

"She's lovely."

The little man nodded. "Kismet will take good care of you."

"Kismet?" Christa couldn't help but smile. With a name like that, the two of them were meant for each other.

The man led Kismet out of her stall and saddled her with graceful efficiency, then gave Christa a boost onto the horse's back. "Don't wander too far. The bulls have been moved in closer than they usually are."

That gave her pause. "Bulls? How much closer?"

"You needn't worry. If you stay out of the pastures you won't be bothered."

Ever since Christa had read Ernest Hemingway's *Death in the Afternoon*, bulls had fascinated her. The way he had described them, they sounded majestic and beautiful, and she would love to see one close up. "Which direction are they?"

"Toward the south."

"Thank you." She paused for a moment. "I'm sorry. I don't know your name."

"Hector."

She smiled down at him and squeezed the horse gently with her knees to get her going. "Thank you, Hector. I'll be back in a little while."

"Remember what I said," he called after her. "You can get into a lot of trouble on ranches if you don't know where you're going."

But Christa and the mare were already out of earshot.

The little mare ran like the wind, but her strides were long and graceful, and Christa found that it was surprisingly easy to keep her seat. They stayed on the road at first, or rather the tire tracks in the grass that made up the only road out here, but after a while Christa wanted to explore a little. There were closed gates set in the white fence—a rolling fence that stretched as far as the eye could see—every several hundred yards. Christa dismounted at the next one they came to, unlatched it, walked Kismet through and fastened the gate behind her. At a much slower pace, they headed over the unmarked pasture.

It was beautiful. No wonder Mark had fallen in love with Brazil. Every once in a while Christa would stop the horse and just gaze around. The grass was long, almost to Kismet's knees, and thick, waving gently in a cool breeze. Banana palms dotted the countryside, giving an exotic look to everything.

They moved on, but stopped when they reached the top of a small hill. Far in the distance, Christa spotted something dark dotting the landscape, and she smiled. "I think we found them. Now what do we do, Kismet?"

The mare strained forward a little against the reins, almost as though she were answering the question, and Christa smiled down at her. "So you're an adventurer. All right. We'll go slowly, but at the first sign of trouble it's up to you to get us out of here. Preferably with me still in the saddle."

They made their way down the slope of the hill and had started to cross the grassy plain that stretched out before them, when Christa noticed someone riding toward them. They were still so far away that she couldn't make out anything about him—or her—but Christa stopped and waited.

As the rider drew nearer, she saw that it was a man in a flat-brimmed hat dressed in the bright, traditional clothes of a South American cowboy. His saddle was ornate, with the leather carved and silver inlaid wherever it could be. It must have weighed over a hundred pounds, but the enormous horse it was on could handle the weight with ease.

The man, who looked to be in his sixties, stopped a few feet from Christa. "Who are you?" He asked in Portuguese.

"Christa Fraser, Mark Fraser's sister."

"What are you doing out here?"

"Exploring the ranch a little."

"You should turn back."

"I will if you say so, but actually, I was hoping to get a little better look at the bulls. Is that possible?"

He looked at her curiously. "Most women prefer avoiding them."

"I'm not most women."

"Apparently."

"And if you can ride with them without being attacked, why couldn't I?"

"Because I know what I'm doing and you don't."

Her friendly smile flashed. "Then teach me."

"You're making this very difficult." He studied her thoughtfully for a moment and came to a decision. "All right. You may return with me to the herd. But you will stay on your horse and do everything you're told."

"Okay."

"Come." He turned his horse and headed back toward the bulls. Christa took a suddenly nervous breath and followed, wondering what on earth she was doing here. This was all Hemingway's fault.

Her guide, whose name she finally found out was Joselito, led her to within a hundred yards of the herd. He stopped and drew Christa and her horse close beside his own. "Well?" he asked as they watched the black beasts grazing, along with twice as many oxen, in the long grass.

The first thing that struck Christa was their dignity. Their presence. One of them lifted his great head and watched her almost in the same way Christa was watching him. It was eerily human. The lump of muscle on his back was flat for the moment. She knew from her reading that the only time it was raised was when the bull felt threatened or wanted to attack. She also knew that when aroused, this calm bull was capable of lifting a horse and rider and tossing them ten feet through the air.

And she was sitting here in a staring contest with one.

"How old are they?"

"These are babies. Most are two or under, though we have a few older ones. That big fellow over there—" he pointed to the one who was staring at her "—is almost three."

"When are they considered full grown?"

"At three and a half or four, though most toreros prefer them younger than four. Bulls are smart when they're young, but when they get older, they're very smart and hard to beat."

"Are bullfights here like the ones in Portugal?"

"That's right. They're fought from horseback, and the bull is never killed in the ring."

The one who'd been staring at Christa went back to chewing, but he was still watching her. She found it interesting that these creatures were so calm as they moved about with the oxen, yet she knew that if one got separated from the herd, he'd blindly attack anything that moved.

The sound of horns clashing against horns rang out, and Christa turned her head sharply to her right. Several hundred yards away two bulls were fighting. It was fascinating, like watching Errol Flynn fighting with a sword. Parry, thrust, jab, and with all of their enormous strength behind each movement.

"Won't they hurt themselves?"

Joselito shook his head as he watched with her. "Not usually. This is how they learn to use their horns. It's a necessary part of growing up. Do you see how they use only one horn at a time?"

"Um-hm."

"Bulls are a little like people. Just as we are either right-handed or left-handed, bulls are usually either right-horned or left-horned."

Christa studied Joselito's profile. He talked about the bulls as though they were his family. Which she supposed they were. He didn't just come out here during the day and then go home at night. The range was his home, and the bulls were his only companions.

Joselito was leaning forward on his saddle with his forearm resting on the horn. He looked at the darkening sky overhead and sniffed the air. "I've enjoyed your company, Mark Fraser's sister, but I think you should start riding home. There's going to be a storm soon and I wouldn't want you to get caught in the middle of it."

Christa looked at the sky in surprise. Where only a few minutes earlier there had been sunshine, there were now rolling gray clouds. The temperature had dropped noticeably. "You're right. I should be going." She extended her hand, and Joselito shook it. "Thank you for being so patient with me."

He just smiled.

"Where are you going from here?"

"Over the next few days we'll be moving west."

"Maybe I'll see you again."

"I hope so. Now go, and ride carefully."

Christa took off across the range as fast as she felt comfortable riding. She'd ridden much farther than she'd thought—much farther. After half an hour, night had completely fallen, and a light rain started. Lightning fingered its way high in the sky, far too high to be any threat, but the thunder that rolled across the plain and through the surrounding hills sent a vibration up through the earth that she could feel.

The little mare wasn't frightened. Christa wasn't thrilled, but the mare was fine. When the rain began falling more heavily, Christa stopped the mare and looked around for shelter. It wasn't exactly a good time to sit under a tree, and there were no buildings around.

She patted the horse's neck and sighed. "I suppose we might as well keep going. I don't think we can get any wetter than we already are."

But it was hard. The rain was stinging. Wind gusts nearly took her out of the saddle. And to top it all off, the only time Christa could see anything was when lightning flashed, and this wasn't exactly familiar territory.

Finally the mare had had enough. She simply stopped walking and turned around so that the rain wasn't flying in her face. Christa dismounted and put her arm around Kismet's neck from underneath. "I don't blame you for protesting. I don't even know if we're going in the right direction anymore."

The mare moved her head so that it rubbed gently against Christa's face, as though she understood.

Christa sighed. "I suppose Hector will tell someone I haven't come back to the stables. And then whoever he tells will tell someone else. And then someone will come looking for us." Lightning flashed again, and she looked around. "I just wish we could wait somewhere a little drier than the middle of the road."

But wait they did. Christa was afraid that if she moved from where she was, she'd just get more lost, and it would take longer for someone to find her. So she stood in the rain. And stood in the rain. And watched the water running in rivulets—and at times rivers—down her body.

"Christa!"

She thought she heard something. She shielded her eyes from the rain with her hand and tried to see into the darkness.

"Christa!"

"I'm over here!"

"Keep talking!"

"Is that you, Matteo? I'm over here! Unfortunately I don't know exactly where 'here' is, but that's where I am!"

"Hello." He sat astride his horse with a flashlight, which he aimed up and down the length of her body. And he smiled at her.

Christa couldn't see him, but she knew he was smiling. "What's so funny?"

"You wouldn't have to ask if you could see yourself."

A smile touched the corners of her mouth as she realized how she must look. "I'm a little wet, I guess."

At that, Matteo laughed. "I guess."

"You can't be faring much better, since you're out here in it with me."

"Ah, but you're the one with the flashlight aimed at her," he said.

"Good point."

"I thought so."

"As much as I love bantering with you, I really am pretty miserable. Do you think we could head back home?" Christa asked.

"Your horse or mine."

"Oh, please," Christa said with a groan. "You lead, I'll follow."

"As it should be."

There was a pause. "The wheels are turning, but I can't think of a single comeback."

"Perhaps when you're dry."

"I hope so. I hate letting you have those words as the last."

"Will you get on your horse please?"

"Hey, I'm willing to cooperate." She pulled herself into the saddle. "But Kismet is another story. She's not crazy about this weather. This is her protest stance."

Matteo shook his head, then moved his horse forward and took the reins from Christa's hands so he could lead them. Kismet was still a little reluctant to turn, for which Christa rewarded her with a grateful pat on the neck.

"It's not as easy as you thought it would be, is it?"

Matteo gave a little tug on the reins, and Kismet turned to follow.

Matteo flashed Christa with his light one more time. "You look disappointed."

"I was just hoping she'd hold out a little longer."

The rain had eased up, so they didn't have to shout at each other anymore. Matteo looked over his shoulder at Christa. "Where were you?"

"Looking at your bulls."

Lightning flashed, and she saw his look of surprise.

"Do you disapprove."

"I'm just surprised."

"About what? That I'm alive to tell the story?"

"Surprised that you'd want to look at bulls."

"I don't know why. They're interesting. And so's the man who herds them."

"Joselito?"

Christa nodded. "He's a nice man."

"He used to let me fight the younger bulls when I was little."

"How little."

"Nine." He shook his head. "I spent a lot of time on the ground."

Christa could picture him with his mussed dark hair and determined eyes, trying to stay in the saddle. "I bet you were cute."

"Cute, hell. I was adorable."

Laughter burst from Christa at his unexpected rejoinder, and at the same moment, the rain made a renewed assault. "Can't we go any faster than this? I'm freezing!" she shouted over the din.

"It's your own fault for wandering so far away from the house. Do you have any idea how worried we all were?"

"I'm sorry."

"You should be. Don't do it again."

They rode for nearly half an hour before the lights of the villa came into view through the rain, and rather than riding to the stables, Matteo went straight to the house. "What are you doing?"

"I'm going to take you inside and get you dried off." He dismounted and then helped Christa down. With his hands still at her waist, he looked down at her.

Christa stepped back and his hands dropped to his sides. "I must looked like a drowned mouse."

"A blond drowned mouse."

"Oh, thanks a lot. You're supposed to say something gallant. Something like, 'Oh, Christa, don't be silly. You're lovely when you're wet.'"

"You are."

She smiled. "Thank you."

"Particularly to other wet mice, I'm sure."

Christa's quick smile flashed. "Charm isn't one of your strong points, you know."

"I know." He caught her hand in his and pulled her along behind him as he walked through an open French-paned door into a living room that three of her apartments couldn't have filled. Classical music played softly in the background. Dona Isabella was the only one in the room, and she sat quietly reading a book.

Matteo stopped suddenly, and Christa crashed headlong into his back. She would have fallen into an ignominious heap behind him if Matteo hadn't reached around and steadied her. Dona Isabella looked up over her Ben Franklin glasses in surprise. Surprise that turned to mild disgust as the two of them stood dripping onto the beautiful Oriental rug. Christa peered from behind Matteo and rolled her fingers at his mother, embarrassed. "Hello. Sorry I'm late for dinner."

Dona Isabella tried not to laugh out loud at the bedraggled picture the two of them presented. "I'm just glad you're safe."

"You're very kind. And now, if you don't mind, before we begin to float oack through the door, I'd like to dry myself off. I'm freezing."

"I'll be back in a few minutes," Matteo told his mother as he put his hand in the middle of Christa's back and guided her from the room.

"So will I," Christa added.

"There's no hurry," Dona Isabella called after them. "Every one else has already eaten."

"You are not coming back down for dinner," Matteo informed Christa.

"Why not?"

"You're going to bed."

"Bed? Why?"

"So you don't get sick."

"Oh, Matteo, you don't honestly believe that my future health depends upon whether I go to bed right now. You're supposed to be a doctor, for heaven's sake."

"You can't go to bed right now. First you're going to take a hot bath."

"And then I'm going to join you for dinner."

"You're going to bed."

Christa just smiled at him.

Matteo sighed. "Why do I get the impression that I'm talking to a wall?"

"A wet wall. That's much worse, you know."

They went up the winding staircase. Matteo opened her bedroom door for her and gave her a little push in. "Get out of those wet things and soak in a hot bath."

"With pleasure."

"I'll be back in a little while."

Christa smiled at him, but said nothing.

Matteo's smile faded a little. "You really are pretty when you're wet, you know."

Christa's smile faded, too, as she closed the door after him, then went straight to the bathroom and started filling the tub with steaming water. Her wet clothes slapped against the tile as she undressed. Then she sank with luxurious ease into the sweet, warm water.

Almost instantly the goose bumps that covered her melted once again into smooth flesh. She sank down to her chin in the water and just lay there for a long time, occasionally reaching up to turn on more hot water.

After a long, long soak, she shampooed and rinsed her hair, then stepped out onto a towel and rubbed herself down. She opened the bathroom door a crack and let the steam out so she could see herself in the mirror. Leaving her hair wet, she brushed it away from her face. Back in the bedroom someone, probably the maid, had laid out Christa's white terry-cloth robe. Matteo was leaving no stone unturned. Rather than protest by getting dressed, she simply put on the robe. She hadn't realized earlier just how tired she was. Too tired to eat, really.

With a sigh, she turned out the light in her room and lay on her bed, her hands folded across her stomach as she stared at the ceiling. Someone knocked on her door. Christa's gaze went to the door. She knew it was Matteo. Her lips parted to tell him to come in, but then she closed them over the words and remained silent.

When she heard him walk away, she turned her head and stared at the ceiling again. A tear escaped from the corner of her eye and dropped onto the pillow.

Matteo went downstairs to the room where his mother still sat reading. Her eyes followed him to the bar, where he made himself a drink, and then to the window, where he stood staring into the night.

"I had the cook warm up some dinner for you and Christa."

"Christa's already asleep, and I'm not really very hungry, but thanks, anyway."

She watched him quietly for a little longer. "You know that Christa is completely out of your reach now."

"I know."

"If it hurts you so much to have her here, you could ask her to leave."

A smile touched Matteo's mouth, but there was no amusement in it. "It isn't her presence. It's that she exists at all. No matter where she goes, I'll always know she's out there somewhere when she should be here with me."

"We've really torn your life apart, Matteo," she said softly. "I'm sorry. It was never your father's intention that you be the one to marry Anna."

"I know."

"Perhaps you could offer her the return of her father's holdings. They're probably worth more now than they were when he died."

"They are. And I already signed them over to her, with interest. The money is important to Anna, but being a real part of this family is more important still. I think she's always felt a little like an outsider. She wants the security that marriage to me will bring her."

"That's partly my fault. I've never really felt close to Anna and I'm sure she's sensed that."

Matteo dragged his fingers through his hair. "That's nothing to blame yourself for. And the way I'm feeling right now has nothing to do with you. It's just that there are some times when it's more difficult for me than others." He turned and looked at his mother. "The rain has stopped. I think I'll go for a walk. Good night."

His mother tried to read her book again, but gave up after only a minute and took off her glasses. What a mess things were.

Chapter Five

Christa awoke early the next morning to a loud banging on her door. She rose up on an elbow and squinted at the watch on her bedside table, then looked at the door. "Who is it?"

"Pilar. I'm coming in."

Before Christa could say anything, Pilar threw open the door and walked quickly across the room to give Christa a hug. "I'm sorry I missed seeing you at dinner. What happened?"

"I went riding and got caught in the rain."

Pilar frowned at her. "You look awful."

Christa rolled her eyes and fell back onto her pillow. "If I don't leave here with a complex about the way I look, it won't be the fault of you or my brother."

"He thinks you look awful, too?"

"Pale."

"Well, you are."

"Thank you."

Pilar smiled at her. "Awful or not, I don't know whether I told you this yesterday, but it's good to see you. I really wasn't sure you'd come until I actually saw you on the plane."

"Even after working the whole thing out with my brother?"

"There were variables."

"There still are."

"You're not leaving, are you?"

"I should."

"Bunk."

"Bunk?"

"It's one of your father's words. I need you to help me out around here." Pilar's English was very Americanized from her years in Wisconsin.

"That's what Mark said." Christa pushed her straight hair away from her face and sat up. "What exactly is it that you can't do without me?"

"As soon as you're up and dressed, I'll be more than happy to show you."

"Show me what?"

"Get dressed first, then I'll show you. We have a lot of work ahead of us."

"What work?"

"Getting Mark's and my house ready."

"I thought you'd be living here."

"We will be, in the broad sense of the word. I mean, we'll still be on the ranch, but not in the villa. Matteo's letting us use his house. It used to belong to our grandmother."

"I didn't know there was a place like that near here. What does it need done to it?"

"Everything. And then some. It hasn't been used by anyone for nearly fifteen years. But it has real potential. I know you'll recognize it the minute you see it. Besides, if being around Matteo is so hard on you, this will be a good way to avoid him. It's miles from here."

"You're too kind," Christa said dryly, but with obvious affection.

"Now you hurry up and get dressed. I'll get my car and wait for you out front." She kissed Christa's cheek and hurried toward the door.

Christa shook her head and smiled as she climbed out of bed and threw on another pair of jeans and a white, open-necked sweatshirt with a pink stripe around her chest. "I wonder if I'll ever get to wear the linen," she said to herself as she closed the closet door. She grabbed her purse and a brush and stuck a ponytail band between her teeth. Braiding her hair into a single plait, she ran downstairs and out the front door. True to her word, Pilar was there ahead of her, her yellow sports car's top down, the motor running. She took off before Christa had a chance to shut the door, and Christa looked at her as though she were a crazy woman. "What's the rush?"

"I'm getting married in less than two weeks."

"Not if you keep driving like this, you're not."

Pilar just smiled at her and kept driving. "Wait until you see the house. It's perfect."

"Does it have electricity?"

"Yes and no."

Christa pondered her answer for a moment. "Yes *and* no? I rather thought it was a yes *or* no kind of question."

"Well, it is—usually. You see, the house has it's own generator, but it isn't working right now. One of the ranch hands is good with things like that. He's been working on it, but it needs some new parts. For now, we have to work by the light of day."

She looked at Pilar, sitting there in a lovely silk dress and high heels. "*We* have to work?"

Pilar flashed her a sheepish grin. "Usually it'll be 'we.' But today it's just 'you.' I have a few more things to pick out for the wedding."

"What exactly do you want me to do?"

"Well, I thought I'd leave that pretty much to your own discretion. All of the basic cleaning has been done, but there's a library, and I didn't want the cleaning people to touch the books, so they need to be done. There's already some nice furniture in the house, but—"

"Let me guess. It needs refinishing."

"Exactly. And if you think about colors and fabrics, and let me know what you think could be used, that would be a big help. I'm hopeless at that kind of thing."

Christa eyed her friend suspiciously. If Pilar did anything well, it was decorate.

Pilar glanced at Christa out of the corner of her eye. "Why are you looking at me like that?"

"You're up to something. I know it as surely as I'm sitting here, and I want to know what it is."

Pilar somehow managed to look wounded. "Christa, just because Mark and I did what we felt we needed to in order to get you here, doesn't mean that we're constantly hatching plots. I think that job of yours has made you paranoid. You should quit."

"Of course. Then I can work on refinishing your furniture full time."

Pilar grinned at her.

Christa clicked her tongue and shook her head. "You're shameless."

Pilar parked the car in front of a tree-shaded white Spanish house. It was a little like the villa, only much smaller. This one probably had only ten rooms or so. They walked up baked red clay steps to a railed veranda made of the same red clay. A glider, faded from the sun and squeaking from disuse as the wind moved it a little, hung on one side. Vines that had once just covered the railing and had probably been quite attractive had been allowed to grow wild, until they now covered everything.

Pilar took her in through the large arched front door to the foyer. It was small, but open, which gave it a sense of space. There was a lovely winding staircase off to the right, a miniature of the one in the villa. "Those lead to the bedrooms."

"How many are there?"

"Four." They walked through another arched doorway. "This is the living room."

It was spacious and bright. Like the villa, there was a wall of French-paned doors.

"And over here is the music room."

Christa followed Pilar down the hall to another room, smaller than the living room, but just as bright. Wallpaper hung limply from the walls, ripped in places. A piano, still lovely, was the focal point of attention. Christa played a middle C, and her eyes crossed at the twang that filled the room.

Pilar took Christa's hand away from the keyboard. "Please. I expect to hear dogs howling any minute." She moved quickly on, and Christa followed. "This," she said proudly as she walked into a beautifully paneled room with wall-to-wall, ceiling-to-floor books, "is the—"

"Let me guess," Christa interrupted. "This is the kitchen."

"And wouldn't you feel stupid if I pushed a button and a stove appeared."

"Stupid and amazed."

Pilar snapped her fingers. "Darn. I knew I should have had that installed. Anyway, this is the library, and a lot needs to be done in here. It'll take days just to clean the books, and the woodwork has to be gone over carefully. My family should be ashamed of itself for letting this place go for so long."

The room across from the library was the dining room. The drapes were torn and disintegrating. The wallpaper in here was also peeling away from the walls, and the heavy Spanish table and other furniture desperately needed refinishing.

"I won't even take you into the kitchen—which, incidentally, is where you can find just about anything you need for working. It's unbelievably outdated, and I've already ordered new things to be installed there. They should arrive sometime in the middle of the week." She looked innocently at Christa and smiled.

"Why are you looking at me like that?"

"Like what?"

"Like you know something that I should know."

Pilar lifted her slender shoulders. "I can't imagine what you're talking about."

Christa didn't believe a word she said, but dropped it. "Is there running water?"

"Oh, yes."

"Not yes and no?"

Again Pilar grinned at her. "Just yes, this time." She looked at her watch. "I'm off."

"I could have told you that. How am I supposed to get back to the villa?"

"I'll send someone for you."

Christa somehow had the feeling she was going to be spending the night here, but strangely, she didn't mind. There was something about this place that she really liked. Much more so than the villa. Oh, of course the villa was beautiful, but it was so big that there was nothing personal or warm about it. This house was everything the villa wasn't and never would be, and once it was fixed up, it would be beautiful.

She walked Pilar to the door and watched her drive off, then turned back into the house and stood looking around the foyer for a while, smiling. She really liked it here.

With an almost cheerful hum, she went to the kitchen. Pilar meant what she'd said about supplies. No matter what she chose to do—be it cleaning, refinishing furniture, or gardening—whatever she needed was there.

Christa decided to start in the library, so to that end, she filled a bucket with water and a special wood soap, grabbed a pile of dry rags and got started.

What a process. Each book had to have fifteen years of dust cleaned from it. Shelf by shelf, book by book, she worked for hours, and was amazed at how little progress she seemed to be making. This room alone was going to take days.

"What are you doing here?"

The voice came out of nowhere and nearly startled Christa off the ladder. She looked down to find Matteo standing in the doorway, watching her.

"I have this thing about standing on ladders in other people's libraries."

Matteo didn't smile.

"So Pilar has you working here, too."

"What do you mean by 'too'?"

"She asked me if I'd come by to supervise the men when they installed the new kitchen equipment."

"But she told me it wouldn't be here until the middle of the week."

They both heard an unmuffled truck chugging toward them in the distance. Christa looked out the window and spotted it, then shook her head. "I knew she was up to something."

"Up to what?"

"Throwing us together, apparently. There was a kind of glint in her eyes this morning."

"She thinks we belong together," Matteo explained. There was a pause. "And she's right."

Christa looked down at him. His black hair was a little disheveled, as though he'd combed it by running his fingers through it. He had on natural-colored pants and a deep-blue heavy-knit sweater over a white shirt. "I love your sister, but she had no right to do that. This is difficult enough for both of us as it is."

"She thinks she's helping."

Christa sighed as she climbed down from the ladder. "I know. We'll have to talk to her."

Matteo moved across the room and put his hands at Christa's waist to help her down the last few steps. She closed her eyes for a moment while her back was still facing him, then forced herself to look at him over her shoulder as calmly as though her heart weren't racing at his touch. "Thank you."

Matteo took his hands away.

"Where's Anna?"

"I left her in the city when I came home this afternoon. She doesn't really like the country. She feels as though she's doing penance whenever she has to spend more than a few days here."

"Or perhaps my presence has made her too uncomfortable to stay," Christa suggested.

"I know she's not pleased to have you around, but that's not why she left. This is her natural pattern. Eduardo also preferred the city."

Christa walked over to the window. "The truck is almost here. I suppose we should meet it."

Wordlessly, Matteo left the room. Christa watched from the window as the truck pulled up, and he directed it to the back of the house. The driver ground the gears and went where he was told.

Matteo turned and looked at Christa standing in the window for a long moment, then he lowered his head and followed the truck.

Christa sat on the window ledge and looked around the library with a sigh. If she really threw herself into working on this house, the next two weeks would glide by. And she wouldn't be running into Matteo all of the time. Or Anna.

Christa couldn't help but think about Anna. It couldn't be comfortable for her knowing that her husband-to-be was under the same roof with the woman he really loved.

Not that she felt sorry for Anna. She didn't feel anything in particular for Anna at all. She didn't know her well enough. Not even to hate.

Matteo appeared in the doorway and leaned against the frame as he watched her. "You look lost in thought."

She nodded. "I was just thinking that if I spend time working on this house I won't be running into Anna very often."

Matteo said nothing.

"I think it would be easier for you and me, too."

Still he just looked at her.

Her eyes roamed over his face and came to rest on his mouth. He had a wonderful mouth—well defined. She wanted to kiss him so badly it was a physical ache inside her. "Aren't you going to say anything?"

"I spent most of my morning in São Paolo with attorneys."

"Why?"

"Trying to find out what is required of me legally with regard to Anna, versus what is required of me morally."

"And?" She was almost afraid to ask.

"I have no legal obligations."

Christa looked at him in surprise. "What?"

"The agreement with my father was a verbal one. Add to that the fact that I've returned all her father's assets to her."

She looked into his eyes and a sad smile touched her mouth. "But you're going to marry her, anyway, aren't you."

The muscle in his jaw moved. "My father gave his word."

"Of course." She looked up at him. "I wish you weren't quite so honorable."

"Senhor?" One of the workmen called him from the kitchen.

Matteo looked at Christa a moment longer before rising and leaving the library.

Christa shook her head. She was starting to feel sorry for herself again. A useless emotion if ever there was one. With renewed determination, she climbed onto the ladder and started on the next shelf of books.

A few hours later, Christa heard the truck chugging away. Then Matteo came back into the library. "I'm going back to the house now. Do you want to come with me, or should I come back for you?"

Christa rested her elbow on a bookshelf and let the rag dangle from her hand. "Neither. I'll walk back later."

"It's going to be dark soon."

"I noticed some lanterns in the kitchen."

"I'm going to get you a car so that you have a little more freedom."

"You don't need to do that," she said, smiling at him. "Where would I go? I can get back and forth by walking. The villa isn't that far from here."

Matteo turned to leave, but stopped at the door. "I don't feel right about your being here alone."

"What can happen? Your ranch goes hundreds of miles beyond where we are now. Not many muggers are going to think it's worth the trip."

"I still don't like it."

"I'm a big girl, Matteo."

A corner of his mouth lifted as his eyes took a leisurely trip down her body. "I've noticed."

Her eyes rested warmly on him. "Good night."

"Good night, Christa."

She worked for a few more hours, but then it got too dark. She climbed down the ladder and went into the kitchen to put her things away. The kitchen looked pretty much the same, except now there was a refrigerator, stove and dishwasher. There was still enough light to see around the house a little, and Christa went upstairs for the first time. The bedrooms still had furniture in them, all covered with big white sheets. She went from room to room. One was obviously for adults. Three had been for children, with one of them a nursery.

She sat in the nursery in an old rocking chair she found there and smiled. This was a charming room. Mark's and Pilar's children were going to love it here.

The sun had sunk even farther. Christa went downstairs and out the front door, but she couldn't bring herself to leave just yet. She sat on the porch swing and set it in creaking motion. This place needed a lot of work. Paint was peeling from the porch ceiling. The baked clay floor had some chunks missing. There was no way in the world the house was going to be ready in time for the wedding. It would probably take months to restore it.

Something suddenly came bounding toward her across the porch and leaped onto her. She laughed as her fingers tangled in the collie's long coat. "Hello! What are you doing here?" she playfully asked the dog.

"I brought him," a voice answered.

She looked up to find Matteo looking at her from a few yards away.

"And what are *you* doing here?"

"Taking care of you."

A warm feeling came over her. She never thought she'd enjoy hearing those words. She'd always taken great pride in taking care of herself. But with Matteo, she somehow wanted him to take care of her. To make everything all right.

"May I sit with you?"

She moved over a little on the swing and made room for him, while the collie bounded off after a rabbit he hadn't a chance in the world of catching.

Matteo sat down and his arm brushed hers.

Christa closed her eyes for a moment and moved slightly away from him. But it didn't help. She could still feel his nearness.

"I suppose Pilar already told you that this was our grandmother's place."

"Um-hm."

"I always loved coming here when I was a child. The house was warm and friendly, the way she was."

"I wish I could have met her."

"She would have liked you."

He looked around. "I feel badly about having neglected the place so."

"You?"

"She left it to me. I'm afraid I let it slip to the bottom of my list of important things to do."

"It's nice of you to let Mark and Pilar have it."

"I thought it would give them a little more privacy. I wouldn't want to move into the villa after I married."

"But you are marrying."

He turned his head and his eyes met Christa's. "Not you."

Christa's throat closed. It was a moment before she could speak. "I think we should go back to the villa now."

"Christa—"

She got up. "Please, Matteo. I don't want to talk about this." Her voice was a whisper. "It hurts too much. Let's just go."

"All right." Matteo got up and walked beside her.

Christa stopped walking suddenly and turned to him, wrapped her arms around his neck and buried her face in his shoulder.

Matteo held his arms away from her for a moment, not knowing what to do, and then slowly, with a look of pain that etched his features, he closed his arms slowly around Christa and held her tightly against him, his face in her hair.

They stood like that for a long time in the dark silence. His body was warm against hers. She slowly moved away from him. "I'm sorry."

He reached out a gentle hand and pushed her hair away from her face. "There's nothing to be sorry for."

"I shouldn't have come."

"You were manipulated."

Christa shook her head. "No, I can't really blame Mark and Pilar for that. I'm perfectly capable of saying no."

"Then why didn't you?"

"I think that deep down, I just needed to see you again." Blue eyes rested on brown ones in a long look. "And I stayed because I can't bear the thought that you're going to marry someone else. I somehow thought that if I were here, it wouldn't happen, but if I left, you'd be lost to me forever."

With a groan, Matteo put his hand on the back of her head and pulled her mouth to his. It wasn't a kiss of passion, but more one of the pain of two people.

Suddenly he released her and walked away. "Sometimes," he said in a hoarse voice, "I lie awake in my bed at night wanting you."

He turned to her.

"And then I realize that I'm never going to have you, but the—the need—doesn't go away. You are such a part of me that even now I can't conceive of what my life is going to be like when you're gone. How can I live with another woman when you're the only one I want? The only one I'll ever want?''

There was nothing Christa could say.

Matteo took a deep breath and slowly exhaled. "I'll walk you back to the villa, but then I'm going to leave. You should stay here with your brother and Pilar. I want you to. But I can't take having you near me like this any longer.''

Chapter Six

When Christa and Matteo got back to the villa they found Pilar, Mark and Senhora Damiano having before dinner cocktails in the living room. Pilar, who had been talking nonstop to Mark, grew suddenly silent and watched the two newcomers with something more than a casual interest.

Dona Isabella smiled. "Won't the two of you join us? We're about half an hour away from sitting down to dinner."

Christa looked at Matteo, who looked unsmilingly back at her. She couldn't think of a way to get out of having dinner with the family without appearing rude. "I have to clean myself up first, but that won't take long."

Matteo's arm brushed Christa's as he walked past her. "I have to return to the city tonight." He kissed his mother's cheek. "You know where to reach me if you need to."

And then he left.

Christa's eyes followed him out and remained on the empty doorway long after he had gone, until Pilar cleared her throat and brought Christa back to her surroundings. Christa managed a halfhearted smile. "As I said, I need to change."

Pilar stood up, torn between feeling guilty about deliberately throwing Matteo and Christa together and believing with unswerving faith that she was doing the right thing. Christa was so pale again. "I'll come with you."

"I think I can handle it on my own, Pilar, but thank you, anyway."

"I just thought you might want someone to talk to while you dress."

"There's nothing to talk about."

"But—"

"Really, Pilar. I'll be back in a few minutes."

When she had gone, Pilar looked at her mother, her mother looked at her and Mark looked at both of them. "I don't think we should have brought her here."

"I'm beginning to agree. I just thought that once Matteo and Christa spent some time together, he'd go back to her."

Dona Isabella looked at her daughter with lifted brow. "Is that why you keep arranging for them to be together?"

"Yes. But I'm going to stop now. I can't bear to see the hurt on their faces any longer."

"And there's no reason to do that to them. You're tackling the problem from the wrong angle."

Pilar narrowed her eyes as she looked at her mother. "Don't tell me you're on my side in this. You've always been in favor of Anna marrying one of your sons."

"That was before," she said softly. "There has been enough grieving in this family. I want to see my children happy again."

"So what are you going to do?"

Dona Isabella smiled enigmatically. "If it works, I'll tell you. If it doesn't, we never had this conversation."

"Oh, Mama, that's not fair."

A good-looking man came through the doors at that moment, tugging at the white cuffs of his shirt so they would show below the sleeves of his dark suit. Senhora Damiano rose and walked over to him, looping her arm through his. "Jorge, how is your room?"

The man kissed her on both cheeks. "It's perfect, as usual. Thank you." Then he smiled at the other two in the room. "Hello, Pilar. Mark."

Matteo walked in at that moment. "I can't leave for São Paolo until later. The weather's bad." Then he saw his friend and best man. "Jorge, what are you doing here?"

"I'm taking some time away from my work to do a little writing, and your mother graciously invited me here."

"With the added lure of Christa."

Matteo looked from his mother to his friend. "What about Christa?"

"I explained to Jorge," Dona Isabella told her son, "that we had a guest here who was a single among couples, and Jorge agreed to be her escort. There are several social things coming up and we can't very well leave Christa behind, or ask her to attend alone."

"She has all of us."

"And now she has Jorge."

The muscle in Matteo's jaw moved, but he said nothing.

When Christa got to her room, she stripped, showered, then lay on the bed in her bathrobe for a few minutes and stared at the ceiling in the dim light of her bedside lamp. She kept slipping into the trap of feeling sorry for herself, and she hated it. It was depressing—and worst of all, boring. She was just going to have to pull herself out of this and go on with her life. Matteo wasn't going to be part of her life anymore. That was the way it was going to be whether she liked it or not. This maudlin attitude of hers wasn't going to change a thing.

Or so she kept telling herself.

She tried to take an interest in her clothes, but just couldn't. She ended up pulling out the first thing her hand touched, a pale, pale yellow linen skirt and silk shirt. She brushed her golden hair away from her face and left it without even bothering to look in the mirror before leaving her room and joining the others.

She paused outside the living room door and took a deep breath, put a smile on her face and walked in. "Hello, everyone."

Mark and a nice-looking man she'd never met before both rose. "Christa," Dona Isabella said, "I'd like very much to present Jorge Montegna."

Christa extended her hand. "How do you do?"

"Jorge is an old friend of the family."

Jorge had brown hair and green eyes, with an open, friendly face. It would have been impossible not to like him.

"Now I really am glad I came," he said in English as he raised her hand to his lips.

No one except Dona Isabella noticed Anna standing in the doorway until Jorge looked past Christa. "Ah, Anna. How are you?"

Anna didn't smile. In fact, she didn't look at all pleased to see him. "Hello, Jorge. I didn't know you were here."

"There's no reason why you would. Dona Isabella invited me."

Matteo's mother patted the cushion beside her. "Come, Anna. Sit with me. We haven't talked for a long time."

Anna obediently crossed the room, while Jorge and Christa sat on the couch across from them. Matteo remained standing, sometimes moving to the French-paned doors to look out, sometimes studying the people in the room. But he must have been listening to the conversation, because he responded to things that were being said.

Anna kept looking at Jorge, who kept looking at Christa and smiling. "Matteo spoke to me of you, but I really had no conception of how lovely you are."

Christa met his look with a direct gaze of her own. "Thank you. I needed that. How long have you known each other?"

"Since we were children. Then we both attended the same medical school."

"So you're a doctor, too."

"Yes, but a different kind. I study diseases and try to trace their origins as well as follow their progress."

"You're more of a scientist than a practicing physician."

"Exactly. And I've been doing that for the past several years. Now it's time for me to sit down with my material and try to make some sense out of it."

"That sounds interesting."

"You're being polite. It sounds tedious."

"I honestly wasn't being polite. I enjoy collating research."

He looked at her with renewed interest. "You wouldn't, by any chance, be interested in helping a poor but respected doctor with his work, would you?"

"As much as time allows. I'd like that very much."

"You're hired."

At that moment a white-jacketed man stood in the doorway. "Dinner."

Jorge rose and held out his arm to Christa. "Shall we?"

She put her hand on it. It was strange. She was surrounded by people who cared about her. Mark, Pilar, Matteo, even Dona Isabella, but with Jorge here, she felt as though she had an ally. Someone she could say anything to without being judged or thought ridiculous.

When they got to the dining room, they were seated at a large round table. Anna and Matteo sat directly across from Christa and Jorge. Mark and Pilar were between the two couples on one side, with Dona Isabella between them on the other. There was a heavy silence in the room until Mark broke it.

"You mentioned the bad weather earlier," he told Matteo as he took a bite of salad. "I heard that the river in the valley is very close to flooding."

"How close?"

"Within another two or three heavy rainfalls."

"Have the people who live down there been evacuated?"

"They won't go."

"You'd better send someone to talk to them, then."

"First thing in the morning."

Christa listened with interest. "I didn't know anyone lived there."

"They're retired employees from the ranch and their families," Matteo explained. "Some of them had nowhere to go after they retired, so we let them use the land for farming. The valley is the most fertile, and that's where they settled."

"Why won't they leave if the river is so close to flooding?"

"Their crops. They've worked months on them and the river could wipe out all that work in a few minutes."

"Couldn't you put sandbags along its banks?"

"We've sent down tons of them, but it's useless. The river's too long and the area we're talking about stretches too far."

The salads were taken away and the next course served.

And so the evening went. Mark and Matteo did most of the talking. Even Pilar was strangely silent. Christa watched the others in the room and became increasingly interested in the way Jorge looked at Anna. And the way Anna looked at Jorge when she thought no one was looking.

When dinner was over, Dona Isabella excused herself and went to bed. Jorge turned to Christa. "Let's go for a walk."

"It's wet out," Anna said quickly. "The winds and rains stopped only a short time ago."

Jorge smiled down at Christa. "I think we can risk it, don't you?"

Christa really didn't want to go for a walk. She felt as though Jorge were playing some kind of game, and she didn't want to be a part of it.

Apparently, Jorge could see the rejection forming on her lips, because he looked at her with a hint of pleading. "Please?"

Curiosity overcame her other emotions. "All right."

Jorge pulled out her chair for her and waved a nonchalant goodbye over his shoulder as he looped his other arm through Christa's.

When they were about fifty yards from the house, Christa stopped walking and turned toward Jorge. "No one can hear us now. I'd like to know what's going on."

"What makes you think anything is?"

"All those looks that passed between you and Dona Isabella during dinner. And my instincts also tell me that the two of you have landed me right in the middle of whatever you're up to."

Jorge smiled at her. "Your instincts are good."

"I know."

He hesitated for a moment as he looked at her. "Can I trust you?"

"What kind of question is that? Do you honestly think that even if you couldn't trust me, I'd tell you?"

"I suppose that was a rather ridiculous question."

"Rather."

"Can we at least keep walking while we talk? I can't stand being still."

Christa fell into step with him. "I'm listening."

Jorge collected his thoughts. "I've been a good friend of Matteo's since we were boys. We've been through a lot together. After we were both in medical school, I came back here with him during a school break and met Anna." He looked at Christa. "I fell in love with her. I asked her to marry me, but she wouldn't."

"Perhaps she wasn't in love with you."

"Oh, she was. But she was more in love with the power and social standing she would have as Eduardo's wife."

"And then Eduardo died."

"That's right, so I came back. I thought things would be different."

"But instead she'd decided to marry Matteo."

Jorge stopped walking and looked at Christa. "I couldn't believe it. You saw tonight how she looks at me. The woman is in love with me, and yet she's determined to marry Matteo."

"She's a practical woman."

"Not really. Not deep down. You don't know Anna."

Christa pushed her blond hair away from her face. "Look, if you're expecting me to get all misty about you and Anna, I'm going to disappoint you. You're right, of course, I don't know her very well. But what I do know is that even though she knows how Matteo and I feel about each other, she's going to marry him. Not because she loves him, but because she loves what he stands for."

"You sound bitter."

Christa sighed. "I don't mean to. In fact, I'm trying very hard not to. It's just that I feel so helpless."

"But that's the point."

"I'm sorry. You've lost me."

"You're not helpless. I'm not helpless. Dona Isabella made me see that when I spoke with her earlier."

"I'm still not following you."

"If, as I believe, Anna is in love with me, seeing me with you is going to upset her."

"Oh, no," Christa said with a groan. "Don't tell me you're going to try to make her jealous."

"That's exactly what I intend. But I need your cooperation."

"You're not going to get it. I don't like playing games and that's exactly what this is."

"Even if it means you and Matteo might end up together, after all?"

"Oh, Jorge, I think you're dreaming."

"I have to, Christa. Otherwise I'll have to accept that she's lost to me forever, and I won't do that until I see them walk down the aisle." He reached out and touched her cheek. A cheek that had suddenly grown damp. "Don't tell me you've given up so completely that you've lost all hope, Christa?"

She turned away from him and stared into the night with her arms wrapped around herself. "I don't know. I need time to think about it."

"Time is the one thing we don't have. The wedding is in less than two weeks."

Christa rubbed her hands up and down her arms. "You know, I'd already decided to leave here. I suppose I'm reverting to the way I coped as a child. When a problem got too big, I turned away from it as though it didn't exist."

"Leaving is the worst thing you could do. She should have to look at you. She should have to look at me. If she goes ahead with this marriage, I want it to be the most difficult thing she's ever done."

"But what about Matteo? He's hurting, too."

"And he's going to hurt a lot more if he has to spend the rest of his life without you. There's no divorce here, Christa. Once they're married, that's it. The most you could ever hope to be to him is his mistress."

"I understand that's very common here. Men have whole second and sometimes third families."

"But not Matteo," he finished for her.

Again she sighed. "But not Matteo. I know that."

"Not because of any loyalty to Anna, but because he would never put you in that position. He loves you too much."

"Spoken like a man who knows what he's talking about."

"I do, Christa," he said softly. "Matteo is a good man, but he's always been a little cynical about things like love—until he met you. I saw him when he returned from his parents' anniversary party, and he was a changed man. It was a Matteo I'd never met before. And you were the reason. Now he's much as he was before."

Christa was quiet for a long time. "And what if we do put on a nice show for Anna, and it still doesn't work?"

"Then at least we can tell ourselves that we gave it our best shot. We won't have to spend the rest of our lives asking the question 'what if.'"

She had to try it. Jorge was absolutely right. As long as there was even the remotest possibility that she could have Matteo, she had to try. Christa took a deep breath and turned to him. "All right. You tell me what to do and I'll do it."

"I don't have to tell you anything. We mentioned your instincts earlier. Well, use them. Let them take over. You follow my lead and I'll follow yours. From this moment on, we have to convince ourselves that we're attracted to each other. For my part, that's not terribly difficult."

Jorge smiled at her, and Christa smiled back.

Jorge's smile faded as he looked at her. Pretending with her really would be an easy task.

"What do we do now?"

"Well," Jorge thought about it for a moment, "I think that when we walk back into that living room, we should be laughing and enjoying each other's company immensely."

"And then?"

"We play it by ear."

Christa's stomach fluttered. She was a terrible actress. Her eyes gave her away whenever she tried to dissemble. As a child, she'd never gotten away with anything. All her parents had to do was question her and she crumbled like a cookie.

"Ready?" Jorge asked.

She took a deep breath. "Ready."

"All right. Here we go." He put his arm through hers as they started walking toward the villa. "Tell me a funny story."

Christa thought for a moment. "I can't think of one."

"Neither can I. Are you ticklish?"

"What?"

He moved his fingers against her side and Christa laughed. "You are."

"Stop that!"

He did it again, and again she laughed against her will, but by this time they had entered the living room and all eyes were on them. Christa's smile faded, and she cleared her throat in an effort to appear more serious.

Anna, sitting on the couch with the coffee service in front of her, quietly watched them.

"Anna—" Jorge pulled Christa over to her "—pour us some coffee, please."

Anna's mouth grew a little tight as she did as she was asked. Pilar and Mark watched in surprised silence. Matteo, who was standing off to one side, his shoulder against the fireplace, his arms folded across his chest, studied with narrowed eyes his friend and the woman he loved. He knew perfectly well that appearances in this instance were deceiving. He couldn't help but wonder what his friend was up to—and he knew it had to be Jorge, not Christa.

Christa. Matteo's dark eyes rested on her pale profile. Her shining hair fell slightly forward, and his fingers seemed to have a need of their own to touch it. She laughed at something Jorge said and her eyes automatically went to Matteo. Brown eyes met and held blue ones for a long moment. Then Matteo looked at his watch and straightened away from the fireplace. "I think I can leave for São Paolo now. The weather has cleared."

"Are you going to stay at the apartment?" Pilar asked him.

"Yes."

"For how long?"

"I don't really know. A few days."

"I'll be coming to the city sometime in the next few days. Is it all right if I use the apartment, too, or would you rather I stayed at a hotel?"

"Of course you can use the apartment. I'll only be there at night, anyway."

He didn't look at Christa again, but came over to Jorge and shook his hand. "I'm glad you're here. I hope we can spend some time together when I get back."

Jorge put his hand on Matteo's shoulder. "I hope so, too. We have a lot of ground to cover."

"Anna." Matteo inclined his dark head toward her and then left the room. Less than fifteen minutes later everyone in the room heard the helicopter take off.

Christa looked at Jorge, and he looked at her. "Christa," he said suddenly, "are you tired?"

"A little." She looked meaningfully at Pilar. "Some of us worked hard today."

Pilar grinned back at her, completely unrepentant. "And some of us are going to work hard tomorrow, too. I want you to make sketches of the different rooms in the house and how you think they should look when they're finished."

"Pilar, I'm not that good—"

"I remember how you would do that with our doll-houses when we were younger."

"That was a lot different. And you're going to be living in this house. I think it should reflect your own taste."

"It will, of course. I'll change anything I don't like."

"Then why don't you just do it yourself in the first place?" Christa asked reasonably.

"Because I have too many other things to do. One of which is to get your dress from the dressmaker." She smiled at Christa. "Wait until you see it. I'm going to have the loveliest maid of honor any wedding has ever seen."

Christa walked across the room and hugged Pilar. "I love you. I'm glad you're marrying my brother."

Pilar hugged her in return. "I love you, too. Thank you for being here for me."

Christa straightened. "If you don't mind, I think I'll raid the library for some night reading, then go to bed. Good night, everyone."

"I'll go with you," Jorge told her.

Pilar looked at him with shocked eyes, and he laughed. "To the library, not to bed."

Pilar's cheeks grew pink. "I knew that."

Anna's eyes followed them out of the room, and they both knew it, but didn't say anything until they got to the library. Jorge grinned at Christa. "I think we did well for our first time out."

"Anna's eyes were shooting daggers at me."

"I have that effect on some women." Jorge was quite satisfied with himself.

"I hate to puncture your balloon, but I'm the one who had that effect on her, not you."

"She's jealous."

"I'd say so."

"So if we can just keep it up without being too obvious about it, we'll see what happens."

Christa kissed him on the cheek. "Thank you for talking me into this. You were absolutely right about hope. I feel a lot better now than I did a few hours ago."

"I know. There's nothing worse than having to sit helplessly by and watch things happen that shouldn't." He gave her a little hug. "Sleep well. I'll see you in the morning."

Christa nodded. When the door had closed behind him, she poked through the books until she found one in English that looked interesting.

Then she turned out the lights, but instead of leaving, she turned back into the room and walked to the windows to stare outside. It was an overcast night. No stars shone. The moon was invisible. Rain started again. Thunder rumbled in the distance, but she couldn't see any lightning.

The rain came down a little harder. Christa set the book on the desk and went out through a door near the window. She walked a little farther into the gardens, then stopped and let the rain wash over her. It was a gentle rain. She could smell the earth. The grass. Everything was being cleansed. She closed her eyes and listened to the drops as they hit the wide, shiny, almost plastic-looking leaves of some of the plants and trees that surrounded her. It was a restful sound. The distant thunder rolled gently across the sky, rather like timpani accenting an orchestra's masterpiece. She wondered where Matteo was. If he'd made it safely to São Paolo.

Matteo stepped out onto the balcony of his apartment. Even though it was late, cars still swarmed below. The rain hit him in light drops, and he welcomed it. São Paolo always seemed cleaner after a rain.

He put his hands on the railing and leaned against it. He'd tried to do some work, but it had been pointless. He kept seeing Christa's face. His marriage loomed ahead of him like a nightmare. He kept thinking he was going to wake up, and yet he knew he already was awake.

What was he going to do without her? It was all he could do to keep away from her now.

And how was he going to help her get through this? He knew her so well. She wanted to run, but she wouldn't. She would be there for Pilar. She would be there for her brother.

And she would be there for him, if he needed her. Matteo knew that. And he did need her. Every minute of every day.

Chapter Seven

Three days later, Christa sat alone with the collie on the porch of Matteo's smaller house, making the sketches that Pilar wanted. Jorge had walked over with her that morning for appearance's sake, but had gotten bored with the sketching and wandered off for a few hours until she was finished.

She kept trying to push Matteo out of her thoughts, but he kept forcing his way back in. He hadn't come back from São Paolo since the night Jorge had arrived, and Christa had missed him—had missed at least being able to see him.

She heard a horse coming toward the house and turned on the porch swing to see who it was. Anna sat there, looking elegant and straight. She stopped the horse near the side of the porch and looked at Christa, who sat on the swing with her legs crossed and a sketch pad on her knees. Then Anna looked around the rest of the porch and grounds as though searching for someone.

"Jorge went for a walk," Christa explained.

"You'd think he'd get enough of walking by coming out here with you. Why don't you ride a horse here when you come?"

"Because then the only one getting any exercise is the horse."

"That makes sense." She seemed unsure of herself. "Do you mind if I join you for a little while?"

"Suit yourself."

Anna climbed off the horse and stepped onto the porch, perching gracefully on the railing as she watched Christa sketch. "It looks nice."

"Thank you."

Anna's fingernails drummed against the railing again and again, tapping out the same beat, until Christa looked up from her pad and just stared at those annoying fingers.

Anna looked from Christa to her drumming fingers and promptly stopped. "Sorry." She left the railing and began to pace. First she went to one end of the porch and then walked back to the other, her riding boots clicking on the baked clay.

Finally, after five minutes of watching her walk back and forth, Christa set the pad beside herself on the swing with the pencil on top of it. "What's wrong, Anna?"

"Nothing, why?"

"Because you've only been here ten minutes, and you're making a nervous wreck out of me."

"Am I? Sorry."

"Is there something you want to talk about?"

Anna opened her mouth to speak and then closed it again. "No."

Christa waited, because she knew something was coming.

Finally, after an obviously vigorous debate with herself, Anna turned to Christa. "I want to know what's going on between you and Jorge."

Jorge had been right. "I see. Well, to put it bluntly, I don't think that's any of your business."

"All right. It's none of my business. But I still want to know."

"He's a nice man," Christa said, watching Anna closely, "but, then, you're already aware of that."

Anna was silent.

"Actually, I'm glad you're here," Christa told her. "I think it's time we had a talk."

"I don't suppose I need to ask what about."

"I don't suppose you do."

Anna brushed a thread from her riding pants and then leaned against the railing again. "I'll go first, if you don't mind."

"By all means."

"I have no apologies to make to you. My father and Matteo's father agreed that I would marry into the Damiano family."

"No matter what the cost."

"It's my right. You don't know the customs of this country. What we're doing isn't unusual."

"I realize that, Anna," Christa said quietly. "Why is it so important to you to become a Damiano?"

"It's hard to explain."

"Try, please. I need to understand."

"You honestly don't know, do you, just what a powerful family they are. They can do anything, buy anything. They can go anywhere and be treated with respect."

"And that's important to you."

"It's the most important thing in the world."

"Do you have any idea what a sad comment that is on yourself, Anna?"

"That's your opinion. But I've been waiting for this for five years, and I'm not going to let anything spoil it now. I'm sorry if you're being hurt by this, but that's simply the way it has to be."

At that moment, Jorge came up the porch steps and saw the two women there. He immediately came to Christa and kissed her cheek. "How are you doing?"

"I'll be finished soon."

Then he turned to the other woman. "Hello, Anna. I heard the last part of what you said, and I take leave to disagree."

"You usually do."

"Nothing has to be. You're in control of your own destiny. And that of several other people at the moment. And I'll tell you something else. If you think that Matteo is going to suddenly fall in love with you someday, you're very much mistaken. You're making a choice, not a compromise. You're choosing one man's power over another man's love, and you're going to be the loser in the end."

"As you said—" Anna straightened away from the railing and headed down the steps to mount her horse "—it's my choice." She looked at Christa. "I really am sorry. If it hadn't been for Eduardo's death, none of this would have happened."

"Almost none of this," Jorge told her.

Anna looked at him for a long moment, then turned her horse and galloped off.

Jorge shook his head and sighed. "It's an act, you know. Inside she's a lot more frightened than she's letting anyone see."

"I'll have to take your word for it. But there's one thing I think you're right about."

"What's that?"

"Anna didn't come out here to talk to me. She came to see what the two of us were doing."

Jorge smiled. "Progress."

"A little."

"So—" Christa picked up her sketch pad and pencil and stood up "—where do we go from here?"

"I guess we'll have to see where the evening takes us."

They started the walk back to the villa and got there about an hour later. Just in time to have Pilar run into the courtyard the moment she spotted them.

"Go change. We're going to São Paolo."

"Why?"

"Because we're all going to have a fun night out for a change. You included, Christa."

Christa thought of Matteo, who'd gone there to get away from her. "I don't think so Pilar. Perhaps another time."

"Not another time. Now. And you're going. Please, Christa. Jorge will end up being odd man out if you stay behind."

"Not if he stays here."

"Is Anna going?" Jorge asked.

"Of course."

"Then, if you don't mind, Christa, I'd like to go."

"Of course I don't mind. I hope you have a nice time."

"We can't leave you here all alone," Pilar protested. "Even Mama will be gone for the night."

Christa laughed at her. "I think I can handle it. In fact, I welcome a chance to have a quiet evening all to myself."

Pilar kissed her cheek. "All right. We'll see you tomorrow in the afternoon, then. Come on, Jorge. You have to change and pack a few things."

"Coming, coming." He followed her into the villa while Christa sat down in a chair and opened the sketchbook again. She wasn't really sure how long she sat there, but night was falling when she heard the sound of a helicopter landing. She didn't think much of it. Between that and the plane, that's how almost everyone got around, including the employees.

Christa leaned back in her chair as she closed the sketchbook, and sniffed the air.

"It smells like rain again."

Christa's heart leaped at the sound of that voice and she turned to find Matteo standing behind her. "I was just thinking that. What are you doing here?"

"How quickly people forget. I live here."

"I mean the others all went to São Paolo to meet with you for dinner and nightclubbing."

"I didn't know that. No one called. Why aren't you with them, Christa?"

"You went all the way to São Paolo to get away from me. I thought it would be inconsiderate of me, to say the least, to follow you there."

He sat next to her.

"Are you going to go back?"

"No. I can't think of anything I would rather not do than go nightclubbing." He inclined his dark head toward the sketchbook. "What are you doing?"

"Helping Pilar to decorate your grandmother's house."

"How's it going?"

"Fine. It's a joy to do, actually. I think if I could pick any home in the world that I'd like to live in, that would be the one. It has a lot of character."

"Then the house would suit you beautifully."

Christa smiled, but couldn't meet his gaze. "Thank you. That's a lovely thing to say."

"It's a lovely thing to be able to say. What's Pilar going to do with the sketches?"

"She said she was going to turn them over to a decorator and tell him to recreate them in the house as faithfully as possible." Christa forced herself to look at Matteo. "This is a terribly stilted conversation we're having. Perhaps it would be best if I just went to my room."

"It won't help."

"Out of sight, out of mind."

His eyes roamed slowly over every inch of her face. "Never," he said softly.

Christa closed her eyes for a moment, then opened them again. "Have you had dinner?"

"No."

"Would you like me to fix you something? I don't think the cook is here."

"I can prepare my own dinner."

Christa looked down again. "Oh."

Matteo reached across the short distance between them and raised her face to his. "I'm sorry, Christa. I keep doing that to you. I don't mean to hurt you."

"I know."

"We'll both fix dinner."

She took her chin from his hand and stood up. "I'd better get my sketches inside. I think I felt a drop of rain."

Matteo looked up at the darkening sky. "I hope not. The river can't take anymore."

"Have the people in the valley moved to higher ground?"

"They won't. I think they honestly believe that by staying they can somehow prevent the flood and save the crops they've worked on so hard and for so many months."

"Can't you force them to leave? It's your property, and it would be for their own good."

"No. This is something they have to do on their own. And they will—soon. They'll have to."

Another drop of rain hit Christa, and Matteo rose and put his hand under her arm to guide her into the house. His touch burned through her, and she moved away as soon as she could without appearing rude. "I'm going to my room for a moment. I'll be right back to help with dinner."

Matteo inclined his head and then watched her as she walked from the room. The muscle in his jaw tightened, and he dragged his fingers through his hair. He had never felt so helpless in his life. He was used to having control. He hated this. He hated the pain he saw in Christa's eyes every time he looked at her. Every time he touched her. But there was nothing he could do about it.

He went into the kitchen and got out the makings for omelets and salads.

Christa stood in her room, looking at herself in the mirror. Once again her cheeks had color. Once again her eyes were luminous. And once again she wanted to run away.

But once again she didn't. She ran a brush through her hair and went back downstairs. By the time she got to the kitchen, the omelet was nearly finished. Matteo pointed to the lettuce and Christa quickly fixed two salads.

Thunder cracked overhead. Christa's hand with the knife in it stopped in mid-tomato slice as she listened. "That sounded very close."

Matteo listened also as yet another crack split the damp silence.

"Where does Joselito go when there's a storm like this?"

"He stays on the range. He has to."

"That's awful."

"That's his job. And if you were to ask him, he'd tell you that there isn't anything he'd change about it. Herding bulls is a way of life. His father and grandfather did it before him. His sons will do it after him."

Christa finished the salad and put it on a table that was set near a window in a corner of the kitchen. Matteo followed her with an omelet he'd cut in two and put on separate plates.

As Christa sat across from him, she looked up and caught his eyes on her. "It looks delicious."

"Thank you."

She lowered her eyes. "I'm trying very hard to behave naturally around you, but it isn't easy."

"Not when behaving naturally—for us, at least— means touching. And kissing. And loving," he said softly.

She nodded.

His gaze rested on her downcast face. With a long breath, he pushed his omelet away. "I'm not as hungry as I thought."

"I'm not, either."

"I think I'll go into the library to do some work and then go to bed."

"Good night."

He looked at her for a long moment. "Good night."

After he'd gone, Christa poked at the omelet with her fork, but finally pushed her plate away, as well.

That was it. She'd finally had it. No matter how much she wanted to see her brother married, or how much Pilar needed her, she couldn't take this any longer. Tomorrow she was leaving, and she wouldn't be coming back.

She went upstairs and undressed. She could hear the rain outside and opened her windows so she could hear it better. The weather here was unpredictable. Some days it was so cool she needed a sweater, and some evenings, like this one, it was sultry. She put on a soft cotton nightgown that was old-fashioned in its modesty and simplicity and lay on top of her covers while the breeze gently lifted the curtains and washed over her body.

She hadn't felt happy for so long she was beginning to wonder if she ever would again.

But she did feel a little better now that her decision had been made. Or perhaps "better" was the wrong word. She felt more at peace than she had for a long time. A decision had been made. Now all she had to do was follow through.

Her eyelids slowly drifted down and she slept, deeply and dreamlessly.

Sometime later a loud noise outside woke her. The thunder was back. Lightning streaked her room with light and thunder cracked and rolled overhead, deafening in its intensity. Christa's heart was hammering the way anyone's heart would when awakened suddenly from a sound sleep.

It cracked again and she hugged her knees to herself. She had never been afraid of thunder before. Why was she afraid of it now? It was just a noise.

Just a noise. Like the artillery fire that had killed people she knew. That had killed a person standing next to her two weeks before she'd come here.

Christa got out of bed and looked into the hallway. It was dark. Matteo must have already gone to bed. She padded down the hall to his room and raised her hand to knock, but then let it fall to her side. Going to him now was the worst thing she could possibly do for either of them.

So she turned around and went downstairs into the living room to pour herself a drink. She turned on a small light behind the bar until she found the dry sherry, poured some into a brandy snifter, then turned the light out again and went to sit on the couch and look outside.

The lightning was so bright and so frequent that it was almost like daylight. And the thunder was one crack after another, each without giving the other a chance to roll away.

"Christa?"

She turned to find Matteo standing in the doorway. He had turned on a light in the hall, and it outlined him from behind as he stood there in his jeans and no shirt. "I'm here," she called out.

"Are you all right?"

"I'm fine. I was a little frightened."

"Why didn't you wake me?"

"I didn't think it was wise."

He walked across to the bar, leaving the living room in darkness. "Can I get you something?"

"I already did, thank you."

He poured himself a drink, then joined her on the couch.

"I don't think I've ever seen a storm this violent," Christa said as another flash of lightning lit the sky.

"This is the one that's going to put the river over. I should get started out there."

"You can't go out in this."

Christa felt his eyes touch her in the darkness. "I'll wait a little while."

He finished his drink and set the glass on the table in front of them, then rose. "I'm going back to bed. You should, too."

"I'll be up in a minute."

The light went off in the hall. Christa finished her sherry and set the glass on the table, then got up and headed for the door.

"Christa, I forgot—"

She hadn't heard or seen Matteo coming back and ran right into his chest. His bare chest. She heard him gasp at the contact. His arms automatically closed around her to keep her from falling, but instead of letting her go, he held her against him. Christa's whole body stiffened in resistance.

"Oh, God," Matteo whispered in Portuguese. "I shouldn't have come back."

Christa's hands were against his chest. She felt the smoothly muscled skin beneath her fingertips and her body unconsciously relaxed a little.

"I just realized," she said in a soft voice, "that I've never touched your skin before. I've never even seen you without your shirt, and yet I feel as though I know you so intimately that we've made love."

"I know. Just as I know every curve of your body without ever having explored them."

"Make love to me," she said softly.

She felt him take several breaths. "Right now, I want you so badly it hurts to breathe."

"Make love to me," she said again. "Just once."

"I told you that I can't make love to you and then let you go."

She kissed his shoulder, lightly caressing it with her mouth, and moved across his chest.

"Christa . . ."

She kissed his throat and up the side of his neck until she found his mouth. His lips were unmoving beneath hers for a moment, but then he moaned and tangled his fingers in her hair. His tongue probed the depths of her mouth as his hand moved over the soft cotton of her nightgown down to the curve of her spine, holding her close against him. Her own hands moved over his smoothly muscled back.

Matteo stopped kissing her suddenly and looked into her eyes. Then he gently kissed her mouth and looked at her again, as though he couldn't quite believe that she was the woman with him. He kissed her lightly several more times like that, each time looking at her, until his mouth finally covered hers completely in a kiss of such tender yearning that a tear spilled onto her cheek.

Matteo kissed it away. "I love you." Then he lifted her into his arms and started up the stairs.

Sounding as loud as the thunder, someone hammered on the door and yelled at the top of his lungs. Matteo looked at Christa, a half smile twisting his mouth, and held her against him for a moment before setting her down and walking to the door.

A man stood there, drenched, and talking in excited Portuguese. Even Matteo had to tell him to slow down so that he could understand him.

He was one of the farmers. The river wasn't going to hold much longer, and they needed help to get everyone out of there, particularly with the children. He even turned to Christa. "Please," he said in Portuguese, "you must help us. We have no time to waste."

Matteo was suddenly all business. "Christa, fix the man a drink or a cup of coffee. I'm going to get dressed, throw some things in the Jeep and go back with him."

"I'll come, too."

"No. It's too risky. You stay here, and when the others come back tomorrow, explain where I am."

"No."

He lifted an expressive brow. "No?"

"No. I'm going with you whether you like it or not." She hit the wall switch to turn on some lights, but nothing happened. The storm had knocked the power out, which should have come as a surprise to no one. She turned to the man and politely explained where he could find a drink if he so desired, then followed Matteo up the stairs to dress.

She came back down not much later than he, in jeans, sneakers and an oversize shirt. She couldn't find a band to hold her hair back in her dark room, so she left it hanging loose. She found Matteo in the kitchen, packing boxes with canned goods and a few things from the refrigerator, and she helped him with that, running into the living room and getting the waiting man and a few bottles of brandy.

Matteo came in from packing the Jeep and stood in front of her. He didn't touch her, yet she felt as though he had. He had to speak loudly because of the noise of the storm. "Are you sure you want to do this? You know what it's like outside."

As though to emphasize his very point, lightning struck a tree not a hundred yards from where they were standing.

"I know," she yelled over the driving rain.

"All right. You were warned. And since you're coming, you might as well take a different Jeep so we'll have extra transportation. You never know what might happen. And we can use the extra room for hauling tents."

"Tents? Isn't that rather flimsy shelter for this kind of weather?"

"I offered to build them something more substantial months ago and was turned down. Tents will have to do for now."

"All right. Where are they? I can start loading them. And for that matter, where's the Jeep you want me to take?"

"I'll drive it around as soon as I get this one packed with the food." He signaled the man who had come for help to start loading things.

"What about medical supplies?" Christa asked.

"I've got a box of those, but I don't think we're going to need them. Mostly we'll be dealing with raw nerves and shock. Floods are horrible ordeals to their victims. And if these people lose their crops, which they probably will, then they've lost everything. Aside from the small pension they get from the ranch, the crops are their only income. They don't have anything to fall back on."

"No wonder they've been so reluctant to leave their homes."

He looked at Christa for a long moment. "It's a different world from our nice, safe one, isn't it?" He picked up a box and started out the door.

Chapter Eight

Matteo loaded Christa's Jeep for her. The other man had already taken off in his own car. When they got to the last box, Matteo turned to her. "You follow me. Stay right on my tail. It's easy to get lost in the valley, and even easier in this weather."

"I'll keep you in sight the entire way."

Still he hesitated. "I don't think you should be going. Something could happen to you."

"Nothing is going to happen. I'll do everything I'm told, I promise."

He leaned forward and rested his mouth against hers. Matteo had an uncomfortable feeling he couldn't explain, but he really could use her help. His best guess was that there were some ten children there whose parents were going to be in no condition to offer them comfort. Christa could offer an extra pair of secure arms, not to mention a helping hand. Without another word, he put the last box into her Jeep.

Christa dashed out into the rain and got into the Jeep as fast as she could, but was still soaked to the skin before she clambered behind the wheel. The motor was already running. All she had to do was adjust the seat and turn on the headlights, and as soon as those went on, Matteo took off.

It was very, very difficult to see. Every once in a while she had a clear view of his red taillights, but just as often, the rain was so heavy it made everything a blur.

The road was muddy. A few times she felt the Jeep slip and slide, but somehow she always managed to get it back under control. The driving was the most difficult she'd ever done and after half an hour of intense concentration, the back of her neck ached and her eyes were burning from trying so hard to see.

The windshield wipers were practically useless. She could hear the rain pounding on the roof and bouncing off the hood. The engine was working hard, and she had to change gears a lot. She hadn't driven a stick shift in years. Every once in a while she'd hear the gears grinding as she shifted. She'd grimace and try to do better the next time.

The farther they went, the bumpier the ride got. They hit some stretches that were so cratered Christa wondered if they'd been bombed.

After an hour and a half, they got to a reasonably level area, but there were minor overflows. They were getting closer to the river. The front wheels of her Jeep would hit the overflow, and muddy water would spray off to the sides like wings.

Then she hit one and the Jeep ground to a halt. She tried to back it up, bit it wouldn't budge. Then she tried to go forward. Nothing. Matteo's taillights had already disappeared. She pressed the horn, and it let out a weak little beep that wouldn't have caught the attention of a blue jay.

Great.

With terrific misgiving, she opened the door and looked at the ground. Ground? It was more like a muddy creek, and her wheels were lodged in it.

Well, there was nothing to do but get out for a closer look. With a wrinkled nose, she lowered herself into the water. It rose halfway up her knees. It was disgusting. Wet was one thing. Muddy was quite another.

She sloshed her way to a front tire and dipped her arm in front of and then behind the tire to find out why it was stuck. There didn't seem to be anything there, so she sloshed her way to the other front tire. That one seemed to be sunk deeper, as though it had dug itself in. "So you're the culprit." She pulled her arm out and kicked the tire.

Lightning streaked overhead, and Christa suddenly realized what a wonderful target she was, standing here like this. Once again she made her way around the

Jeep to the driver's side and climbed in. She rocked the Jeep back and forth and back and forth, as if she were stuck in the snow. But nothing happened.

She glimpsed headlights coming toward her through the rain. Matteo had come back for her. Feeling much better about things, she jumped down from the Jeep and made her way toward him through the water.

"What's wrong?" he yelled through the noise of the storm.

"I'm stuck!" she called back. "I think I need a push."

"I don't want to bring my Jeep back into that. We might both end up stuck. You get behind the wheel, and we'll try to rock it out."

Christa nodded and waded back through the water to her Jeep, with Matteo following.

He put his shoulder to the back of the Jeep. "Go forward for short bursts of time when I tell you to start. Ready?"

"Ready."

"Start."

Christa did. She accelerated, then stopped. Accelerated, stopped. And finally, the fifth time she did it, Matteo managed to push the Jeep out of the rut, and it shot forward. She stopped it next to his and then got out. The wind was picking up again, she noticed, and the trees were waving and bending wildly. It was almost like being in a hurricane.

Matteo came out of the creek, now as drenched as she was. "I'll turn around and you try to stay behind me. If you can't, for any reason, honk."

"I tried that. The horn isn't loud enough."

"Then flash your lights."

"All right."

"Let's go."

He made a U-turn with his Jeep and passed Christa. She fell in behind him.

Nothing more happened on the last half-hour of the drive, except that things got more and more difficult because of the high winds. A few times it felt as though the Jeep were going to be carried off, and it did in fact get knocked off course a bit.

Finally the Jeep ahead of her stopped, and so did Christa. She climbed out of her Jeep and got hit with yet another solid sheet of rain. She was beginning to have feelings of nostalgia about being dry. A gust of wind hit her and knocked her to the ground. Matteo was next to her in an instant, offering her his hand.

"Where's the river?" she yelled.

"About fifty yards that way." He pointed.

She looked in that direction, but between the dark and the rain, she couldn't see anything, and the lightning seemed to have given up for the night.

"What do you want me to do?"

"You work on getting the children evacuated. Get them up on higher ground and set up the tents. It's going to be hard in this wind, but some of the men can help you. If you do it right, the tents will stay up."

"No small challenge."

He gave her a wet hug. "And you take care of yourself."

"You, too."

She ran toward one of the houses while Matteo headed for the light of some lanterns he'd noticed closer to the river. She hammered on the door, and a woman calmly answered it. Christa introduced herself in Portuguese and explained why she was there.

The woman nodded and rounded up her children and one suitcase of belongings.

After they had all piled into her Jeep, Matteo knocked on the window. Christa rolled it down. "What?"

"I'm helping the men do a little more sandbagging. I don't think it's going to serve much purpose, but it's better than doing nothing." He stepped aside and made room for a huge man. "This is Rolf. He's going with you to help with the tents. He'll show you where to go to set up."

"All right. And then I'll be back."

"To this same area," Matteo told her. "I know you can't see in this rain, but the houses are arranged in something of a compound rather than being scattered over large areas." He leaned in through the window and cupped her muddy face in his hands. "You're wonderful."

A smile warmed her eyes, but then he was gone. The big man stood outside her Jeep. Christa looked around, then back at him, and lifted her shoulder apologetically. "I'm afraid there's no room in here for you."

He inclined his head and walked around to the back of the Jeep. A moment later there were two loud thumps, which Christa interpreted as a signal that she could go, so she did. Slowly and uphill. Again there was no road and she hadn't the faintest idea where she was going. Rolf, at one point, jumped off the back of the Jeep and walked quickly alongside it, shouting directions at her in Portuguese until they were finally there.

Then, without wasting a moment more, he hauled the tents out of the back and got to work. She let the children and their mother stay in the Jeep while the first tent was being put up. She couldn't very well turn them out into this mess and force them to stand around in it. About half an hour after he'd started, the tent was done, including a lantern burning inside. The mother got out of the Jeep and hurried her children into the tent. While Christa turned the Jeep around to go back for another load of human cargo, Rolf started working on the next tent.

Christa found her way back down and went to the next house. This went on until she had everyone up the hillside who would go. There were no men in the tents as yet. All of them were still desperately trying to save their crops, even though if the flood didn't kill them, this storm probably would. She didn't see how anything could stand up to this abuse.

The rain changed texture. Where once it had been a drenching sheet, it now became stinging drops. When she got the last of the people up the hill, the mother of the first group came running out. "Have you seen my son's dog? He's little. Only so high," she said in Portuguese, lowering her hand toward the ground so that she measured about a foot for the height of the dog.

"I didn't see any animals."

The little boy came running out into the rain. "My dog, my dog." He was crying, and Christa, who had planned on going back, anyway, promised him she'd look.

And she did. When she came back down the hill, she saw Matteo working with the other men as they passed the sandbags down a line from one pair of hands to the next to the next. She saw in a flash of new lightning why Matteo thought this was an exercise in futility. There was no way they could protect the length of the riverbank from flooding. It stretched much too far. And even if the river swelled over its banks farther downstream, the water would make its way back here with about the same force.

Christa shielded her eyes from the rain with her hand and tried to see beyond her nose. It suddenly dawned on her that she didn't know the missing dog's name, so she just started clapping and calling, "Here, dog," in Portuguese as she walked around the compound.

She tried for nearly twenty minutes and was about to give up, when she heard a faint yelp coming from the direction of one of the houses and followed the sound to one of the scrawniest, saddest-looking excuses for a dog she'd ever seen. He won her over instantly with his huge, soulful eyes.

He was all right, but he was frightened and trying to hide from the storm. Christa walked over to him, talking to him, coaxing him, telling him she was his friend, and finally she picked him up.

Then it happened. She heard something snap and before she knew what hit her, she was pinned to the ground by a tree limb across her legs. She still held the dog, who was now surprisingly quiet. It took a moment for Christa to get over the shock of getting hit like that, then she started yelling. But the wind seemed to pick up her cries for help and throw them back in her face. She yelled until she was hoarse and nothing came out. No one heard her. No one came.

The tree trunk was wedged against something in addition to her legs, which was why she wasn't hurt as badly as she might have been. But she was still on her stomach in the mud, unable to budge the limb and unable to move herself.

She scratched the puppy behind his ears and then let him go. "I think you'll stand a better chance being on your own."

But the dog wouldn't leave her. He was a loyal little thing and just stood next to her, yapping his heart out.

Christa's legs were beginning to hurt. She tried again to pull herself out, using her hands and arms and digging them into the mud to get some leverage, but it was useless. She lay still for a moment and watched the little dog. If only she could send him after Matteo, everything would be fine. ''Where's Lassie when you need her?'' she asked futilely.

Christa heard a noise and grew alert. Even the dog sensed the need to be still while she listened. It was a car engine. And then another. They were leaving! The men were leaving! And no one even knew she was here. She tried yelling again, but once more the wind and rain threw her voice back in her face.

And then it was quiet except for the storm. No more engines.

She tried again to pull herself forward, exhausting herself with the effort. She was in such an awkward position. Both her upper and lower legs were pinned, and she couldn't turn onto her back so that she might be able to move the limb herself. Her hands might as well have been pinned, too, for all the use they were to her.

She had no idea how long she lay there waiting for something to happen. The river had to be close to flooding, or else the men would still be working. When Matteo got back to the camp they'd set up, he was bound to look for her, and someone there was bound to tell him she'd come back here looking for the dog. But who or what would find her first? The flood waters or Matteo?

She didn't have to wait long for an answer. Water began rising all around her. ''Damn,'' she swore under her breath as she arched her back to keep her face as much above the water as she could. The dog was obviously frightened, but refused to leave her, even when the water threatened to submerge him. Christa reached out and grabbed him by the fur behind his neck, then set him on her back.

The water kept rising. The only thing that kept Christa from panicking was the thought that the deeper the water got, the better the chance that the limb would simply float off of her and she'd be free. But it didn't happen, and by the time the water was up to her chin, she couldn't stretch any higher and she couldn't move. The dog jumped into the water and paddled around her, yelping.

Christa stopped struggling as soon as she realized that it wasn't doing her any good. She became aware of everything around her as though it were magnified. The rain as it splashed into the water around her. The numbing cold throughout her body. Her hair as it floated around her face. And the river water as it inched its way over her chin and mouth. She was mad as hell about this. And that's what she was thinking as the water finally closed over her nose.

A light danced off the water around her. "Christa? Christa?" There was a pause. "For God's sake, woman, answer me!"

Then the flashlight picked out the hair floating. Matteo's heart stopped for a moment, but then it was as though he'd been shot with adrenaline as he waded to her. He put his hands under her arms and tried to drag her to the surface, but he couldn't do it.

Forcing on himself a calm he was far from feeling, he ran his hands down her body until he found the limb across her legs. He struggled with it, but it was wedged. He could only lift it a little. He went under the water himself so that he could lift with one hand and free Christa with the other.

All this only took a few seconds, but to Matteo it seemed like a lifetime.

Once he got her to the surface, he was afraid he wouldn't have time to get her onto land. He had no way of knowing how long she'd been underwater. He braced his foot on the limb and raised his knee, then laid Christa's limp body over it so his thigh was under her stomach and her head hung low. He pushed on her back, forcing her stomach to press into his thigh. "Come on, Christa."

She didn't move.

He pressed on her again. "Please, Christa," he said tightly, "come on."

He kept pressing on her, harder and harder, until she finally started choking and ridding herself of the water she'd swallowed.

Matteo closed his eyes for a moment.

"Matteo?" she croaked.

He turned Christa into his arms and held her tightly against him. "You're going to be all right."

Christa wrapped her arms tightly around his neck. "What took you so long?"

He shuddered to think how close he'd come to not finding her at all, and held her even closer. "You're not the easiest person in the world to track down."

She pulled away from him suddenly. "The dog! Where's the dog?"

"I don't know, but right now I'm more worried about you. I'm going to get you back to the camp." He put one arm under her legs and another around her back as he lifted her.

"Please, Matteo, I have to get that dog."

"First I'll take you to the Jeep, and then I'll find the dog, all right?"

She nodded and put her head on his shoulder.

His flashlight was long since gone, but as they walked he thought he saw a movement several feet away, and sure enough, he reached into the water and scooped out one pitiful-looking pup, which he put on Christa's stomach. "Hold on to him. We're not coming back for him again."

Christa laid one hand limply on the dog's wet coat, while she kept the other arm around Matteo's neck. He was having trouble keeping his balance in the rapidly moving floodwater as he made his way to the Jeep he'd left parked halfway up the hill.

He settled Christa onto the passenger seat and, without wasting any effort on words, turned the Jeep around and made for the camp. The little boy who owned the dog ran out to meet them. The dog jumped out of Christa's lap before the Jeep had even stopped and ran straight into the boy's arms.

Matteo walked around the Jeep, plucked Christa from the seat and carried her to an empty tent, then gently set her on the ground. "Don't move until I get back," he ordered.

Christa wasn't about to. Her legs hurt terribly, which she assumed was good, but she wanted to hear what Matteo had to say about that.

He opened the tent flap and stood looking at her for a moment before carrying in the cot, blankets, dry clothes and a medical bag. The first thing he did was cut her pants away from her legs. With gentle and wonderfully warm fingers, he worked his way over her calves and knees and then her thighs.

"You do that well," she said softly.

"So I've been told," Matteo answered without looking up.

She was silent for a moment as she looked at the top of his dark head, bent over her legs. A battery powered lantern sat in the middle of the floor, offering unwavering light, and in that light she saw that he was at least as wet as she was. A tender smile, full of love, touched her mouth as she glanced at him.

Matteo glanced up at her and saw the look. He suddenly reached behind her head with one hand and pulled her mouth tightly against his. Then he rested his forehead against hers and looked into her eyes. "I could strangle you sometimes," he said quietly. "And if you ever put me through this again, so help me, I will strangle you."

"I consider myself warned."

"You should consider yourself damn lucky to be alive."

Matteo moved away from her and started putting things back into his medical bag. "Your legs are fine. They're going to hurt for a few days because they're badly bruised."

He handed her a bottle of brandy. "Sorry, no glasses."

She took a swig and smiled at him. "I feel so bohemian."

"You look so wet."

"And cold."

Matteo tapped the bottle. "Take another one."

She did. "I'm getting warmer."

He took the bottle from her and capped it, then helped Christa to her feet while he peeled the wet clothes from her body and toweled her off with one of the blankets. "It looks like the rain washed most of the mud off of you."

Christa watched him as he did it, amazed by her complete lack of embarrassment.

Then he took a dry blanket and wrapped it around her. "Lay on the cot."

She did as she was told, and he wrapped yet another blanket around her. "This should help you warm up."

"Thank you."

"I'll be back to check on you later."

And he left, taking the lantern with him and leaving Christa in darkness. She took a deep breath and exhaled. Her eyes stared into the dark corners of the tent as she listened to the rain on the canvas. It was nothing more than a drizzle now. The wind was still strong enough to whistle around the tent, but much less powerful than it had been. Christa pulled the blanket around her more securely, but she was still cold.

She closed her eyes tightly and tried to sleep, but she kept thinking about what had almost happened. The more she thought about it, the more frightened she became, until, when Matteo stepped back into the tent to see how she was, she shot up from her cot and threw herself into his arms.

Matteo held her close against him, pulling her blankets up and stroking her back. "Shh," he whispered against her hair. "You're all right now."

"Stay with me."

He hesitated. "I really don't think—"

"Please." She pulled away from Matteo and looked at him with pleading eyes. "Please don't leave me. I need you. Please."

After what was obviously an inner struggle, he pulled her back into his strong arms. "All right. I'll stay with you tonight, and for as long as you need me."

"I'll always need you."

He held her even closer. Then he lay on his back on the cot and gently pulled Christa down with him. Her cheek rested against his shoulder, her arm around his stomach. She arranged the blanket so that it was over him as well.

Matteo's hand moved to Christa's body, bare under the blanket, and gently rubbed her back and arm. Her flesh still felt cold, though she wasn't shivering.

He felt her breath as it touched his chest. "I don't want to sleep now," she said softly.

"Why not?"

"Because in the morning this will all be over. You'll be gone, and there'll be no more nights for us to share."

Matteo moved his hand across her back and held her closer.

"Unless..."

"Unless?"

"Unless you take me for your mistress."

A tender smile touched his mouth as he kissed the top of her head. "I don't want you for my mistress, Christa. I want you for my wife."

"But that's not possible for us." She was quiet for a moment. "I've been doing a lot of reading, and I've spoken to one or two people."

"About becoming my mistress?"

"About mistresses in general. They're very common in Brazil, you know."

"I know."

"And there's no stigma attached to it. Perhaps we could have a family. I read that the word 'illegitimate' was stricken from your language because it's such a common thing, and so accepted by everyone."

"No, Christa."

"But why?"

"I won't do that to you."

"But you wouldn't be *doing* anything to me. It's what I want."

"You don't know what you're saying."

Christa raised up and looked at him as best she could in the dark tent. "I know exactly what I'm saying, Matteo. Anna doesn't want you. She wants your name and your money. Well, she can have all that, as long as I can have you."

"But you wouldn't have me, Christa. Not completely. You'll have to watch me go home to her every night, wondering if I'll be making love to her. Wondering when we'll next be able to be together. And what about your work?"

"I'll quit."

"To do what? Spend your days waiting for a call from me? You can't do that. You're incapable of it, and I wouldn't inflict it upon you."

"Matteo."

He pulled her back to his shoulder. "No, Christa."

"You won't even consider it?" she asked quietly.

"No."

Christa sighed. "I guess that's it, then."

He rested his mouth against her hair. "I guess so."

She moved her body closer to his, and even though Matteo had clothes on, her warmth penetrated them. He hadn't known it was possible to want a woman as much as he wanted Christa. To ache with the need to hold her. To touch her.

They lay very still. Then he heard Christa's breathing turn deep and even, and he knew she was asleep.

His mind flashed back to seeing her hair floating in the water. He held Christa closer to him and buried his face in her hair as tears coursed down his cheeks.

Chapter Nine

Christa lay in the cot with her eyes closed long after she was awake. Matteo was gone. He'd been gone for quite a while.

She rolled onto her back and opened her eyes. The sun was shining outside. She could tell from the warmth inside the tent and the spots of light that got through the canvas. She heard people speaking in Portuguese.

The clothes that Matteo had brought her last night lay at the foot of the cot. She stood up slowly and carefully—he'd been right about her legs hurting. The blanket that was wrapped around her fell to the ground. She stepped into a pair of worn cotton pants that were much too long and big around the waist, and pulled on a man's shirt. She rolled up the cuffs of the pants until they were halfway up her calves and rolled up the sleeves of the shirt, but the pants were still way too big. She held them up with one hand and left the tent in search of rope.

Matteo was the first person she saw, and her heart lurched when he smiled at her. "Do you always look this lovely early in the morning?"

A dimple creased her cheek as she thought of how she must look. "Do you always put your life in peril this early in the morning?"

He inclined his head toward her pants. "Do you need something to help hold them up?"

"A rope or some string, if there's any around."

She watched as he ducked into a tent, and thought that he really looked wonderful. He had on the same clothes he'd worn the day before, but they were miraculously clean—probably because one of the women here had taken the time to wash them. His black beard shadowed his face—something she found surprisingly attractive.

When he came back out, Matteo handed her a length of rope. Christa threaded it through the loops and tied it. "Thanks. How are things in the valley this morning?"

"Wet. The water is still high, but it's starting to recede. We should be able to start cleaning up late tomorrow."

"If it doesn't rain again."

"It's not supposed to."

He looked at her legs. "How are you feeling this morning?"

"They hurt as though I did a few hours of stretching exercises after months of inactivity, but considering the alternative, I can handle it." She raised her head a little and sniffed the air. "What is that wonderful aroma?"

"Breakfast. Want some?"

"Are you kidding? I feel as though I haven't eaten in weeks. Point me toward it."

Matteo put his hands on her shoulders and turned her slightly, then gave her a little shove. "Follow your nose."

She looked over her shoulder at him. "Where are you going?"

"Most of the men are in the valley. I think I'll head down there to see if I can help."

She knew without his having to say it that he'd waited to see how she was. "If you can wait a few minutes, I'll come too."

Matteo lifted an expressive brow. "You don't honestly think I'm going to let you anywhere near that place again, do you?"

"What happened to me last night could have happened to anyone. How could I have known that limb was going to fall on me?"

"You shouldn't have been there at all."

"What was I supposed to do about the dog? If you had seen that little boy's face..."

"The dog, you might remember, was in considerably better condition than you were when I found you last night."

"I couldn't have known that at the time, could I?"

A corner of his mouth lifted. "Do you want to argue about it?"

"I hate it when you take the wind out of my sails like that."

"I know you do."

"But you do it, anyway."

His smile grew. "Now about your going to the valley today."

Christa waited.

"You're not."

She smiled at him and Matteo shook his head. "I should know better than to give you orders. You don't seem to take them very well."

"I'm much more receptive to suggestions."

"Then I politely *suggest* that you stay here."

She didn't say anything.

"Well?"

"I said I was more receptive, not that I would blindly agree. I don't like being labeled an incompetent simply because I got caught up in circumstances beyond my control."

Matteo shook his head. "Go eat."

She smiled at him and walked away. His eyes followed her until she disappeared around a curve in the clearing. He felt as though he had to fill himself with

the sight of her now, because it wouldn't be long before she was out of his life.

Christa found several of the women she'd helped the
night before, sitting in makeshift chairs while they did
needlework in front of a tent. Laughing and running,
a child nearly ran Christa down, but she saw him
coming and sidestepped—not with her usual grace, but
at least she managed to get out of the way.

One of the women smiled at her and invited her to
join them. Christa asked in Portuguese if there was
any breakfast left. They all started talking at once, and
then one of them appeared out of nowhere with a plate
of the most delicious-looking eggs along with bread
that had been toasted over the open fire. Christa lowered herself slowly into the chair and breathed in re-
lief when she finally made contact. Then she smiled at
the woman and dug with relish into the food. And
what wonderful food. It had never tasted so good, and
she savored every single bite.

She inclined her head toward one of the women
who was making something that looked interesting.
"What's that?"

"A seat cover." She held it up so that Christa could
see it better. "It's for one of my dining room chairs."

Christa looked at the intricate, beautiful design that
had obviously taken the woman painstaking hours of
work to accomplish. "That's lovely." Christa set her
plate down and, with a small wince, got up to take a
closer look. "I've always wished I could sew something like that, but I've never had the patience."

The woman, probably in her forties, smiled. "I could teach you. We have a long day ahead of us."

Christa squeezed her hand. "I'm sorry about your houses."

"The houses can be cleaned. But the crops—" She shook her head. "It'll take months to start those over again."

"Matteo will make sure you have help."

"He's already letting us use the land. How much more can we expect him to do?"

"It's not a matter of expecting anything. It's a matter of helping where you can. He's a good man. That's why he's here now instead of safe and dry in his own home."

The woman smiled at Christa again. "Come. I'll show you how to do this." And she took the petite-point canvas and made some stitches, while Christa watched.

And that's how they passed the morning. But there was much to do even in the tent city with children to be taken care of and husbands to be fed. By the time Matteo got back, it was almost dark. Christa saw the headlights of his Jeep and she smiled softly as she walked out to greet him. When he stopped, she rested her forearms in his open window and looked at him. "Hello."

Matteo's brown eyes gazed tenderly at her. "Hello, Christa. How are you feeling?"

"Better than I was this morning."

"Good." He hesitated for a moment. "I was thinking about what you said this morning."

"I said a lot of things this morning."

"I mean about my treating you like an incompetent over circumstances out of your control."

"Ah, that."

"You were right. That's exactly what I was doing, and I'm sorry."

"Does that mean I can help the others with the cleanup tomorrow without having to feel as though I'm disobeying a direct order?"

She was joking, but Matteo didn't smile. "Christa, you have to understand that last night, when I found you, I thought I was too late. I thought you were dead. That you were lost to me forever, and I—for the first time in my life—confronted a situation that I didn't know if I could handle. When some people you love die, you grieve for them—for yourself—and then you go on with your life. But last night, I realized that without you, I have no life. There's no meaning to it. I may not be able to love you freely, but at least I know you're there, and that knowledge fills every void in my life."

Christa's heart was in her eyes. "Just for tonight, can we pretend that we belong to each other? That besides us and the people here with us, no one else exists. I want to be able to hold your hand, and touch your arm, and tell you I love you without anyone else intruding."

"Christa, I don't want to hurt you anymore than I already have."

"Then let me have this night. I won't ask you to make love to me. Just to let me be with you. This one night is going to have to last me a long, long time."

She leaned in through the car window and kissed his beard-shadowed cheek.

Matteo didn't know what to say. He withdrew a little from her, but it wasn't physical. It was more something she sensed.

She backed out of the car. "I think the others are waiting for us by the fire."

Matteo opened the door and climbed out. They started walking side by side, yet not touching. Suddenly Matteo reached out and caught Christa's hand. She looked down at their joined hands. Matteo squeezed it a little. "Smile for me, Christa."

She did, and it was a smile filled with such love that his heart caught.

The women were serving dinner when they got there. It was a kind of stew made from the food that Matteo and Christa had brought. The two of them took their plates and sat on a blanket while they ate. The children were tired from playing all day. Most of them were already in bed, and the few holdouts were snuggled in their mothers' arms, listening to the conversation about what had happened that day and what was planned for the next.

Christa listened intently, and at one point touched Matteo's arm. "Where are you planning to get the necessary tools for the cleanup?"

"I sent a man back to the ranch late this afternoon. He should be bringing whatever we need early tomorrow morning."

Christa finished her stew, then set her plate aside. "What about the crops? Is there anything left?"

"The coffee should be all right, but everything else is completely gone."

"What are you going to do about that?"

He shook his head as he leaned back against a tree and stared out at the starry night. "I don't know. My inclination is to offer them money to help them through this, but they're people with great pride. They won't take it." He turned his head slightly and looked at Christa. "And it isn't just the crops. You should see the houses."

"Can't they be cleaned?"

"They'll have to be. They're without exception thick with black mud. Much of the furniture is broken. Anything fragile is ruined. I'm not looking forward to seeing the women's faces when they walk into their homes tomorrow."

"They're very strong. They can handle it."

The last of the children went to bed. A man brought out his guitar and began playing soulful Portuguese tunes the likes of which Christa had never heard before.

"Come here, Christa."

She moved back so that Matteo could put his arm around her and hold her close to his side as they listened.

After a while, he moved farther down on the blanket and put one hand behind his head, while the other arm was still around Christa. She wanted to be close to him, but tried not to be provocative. For her, the wonderful music with its sensual rhythm was secondary to the man. She snuggled against Matteo, and as it had last night, her hand rested lightly on his muscled stomach. His warm breath ruffled her hair as his hand moved slowly up and down her arm. They must have been like that for an hour, as one by one the others drifted to their tents until everyone was gone and all the lights were out except for the dying fire, fifteen feet away.

Christa lay there, perfectly still, wondering if Matteo had fallen asleep and finally deciding he had. She raised her head from his shoulder and looked down at him. His eyes were closed. His breathing quiet. She could have looked at him all night. She wanted to look at him all night.

She raised her hand and ran her fingers through his thick hair, loving the way it felt. And would have done it again, but Matteo's own hand reached up and caught hers. She found herself looking into his eyes as she lay half on top of him.

He didn't say anything. He didn't have to. With a groan he cupped the back of her head in his hand and pulled her mouth to his as he rolled her onto her back.

Christa's mouth parted automatically to invite him inside. And he entered, exploring her with a slow thoroughness.

Matteo lifted his head and gazed down at her with a look so full of tenderness that he needed no words to express how he felt.

As he continued to look into her eyes, his hand made its way down the side of her body to her thigh and pulled her more tightly against him. If ever Christa had wondered about his desire for her, she need wonder about it no longer. It was there, pulsing against her.

His mouth moved to her ear, and he gently flicked it with his tongue and kissed all around it.

Christa felt a warmth grow inside her and spread like fire. She became lost in sensation, aware of herself only in relation to where he was touching her. His hand moved under her shirt and caressed her waist, moving around to her back and massaging its way up. Then he began to unbutton her shirt, button by button, starting at the bottom and kissing the bare skin of her flat stomach. His mouth moved to her waist, then up to where he undid another button. His mouth explored her skin as though he wanted to know every inch of her body, not just with his hand, but with his mouth.

When he got to the last button, the one that held the shirt closed over her bare breasts, Matteo raised his head and looked at her. His hand gently massaged the side of her breast before he lowered his head and kissed her in soft, ever shortening circles until he found her nipple.

Christa arched toward him with a moan, unaware of anything or anyone but this man and what he was doing to her. Matteo's arm went around her arched back, holding her closer as he kissed her breast more deeply.

Christa tangled her fingers in his hair and pulled his mouth to hers, moving her body suggestively against his, opening his shirt so that her skin was touching his. The movement of his body against hers matched the thrust of his tongue deep into her mouth.

Suddenly he stopped and looked down at her, shaking his head. "No, Christa. We can't."

"Yes, we can."

"I can't make love to you and then watch you walk away."

He raised his body off of hers and gently rebuttoned her blouse, then rolled onto his back with his forearm over his eyes. Christa reached out to him and Matteo obviously sensed her movement. "Don't touch me. All it would take to send me over the edge is one touch from you."

Christa let her hand drop. Her heart was pounding beneath her breast. She ached to have him inside her.

But she knew he was right.

Wordlessly she rose from the blanket and went to her tent, but there was no sleep for her that night.

The next morning, Christa got up as soon as she heard movement from others in the camp. She'd slept in her clothes since she'd had nothing else, and noted with a half smile that she looked fashionably rumpled.

When she came out of her tent, she saw Matteo speaking with another man. He looked up, but didn't smile. "Good morning."

She nodded wordlessly.

"We're leaving for the valley in a few minutes."

"I heard."

"You're welcome to ride with me. The Jeep you drove is down there, but it isn't functioning."

"I'm afraid it got caught in the flood the same way I did. Sorry."

"It's not beyond repair. Don't worry about it."

She nodded. "If you don't mind, I think I'll walk."

"What about your legs?"

"They're feeling a lot better today."

They both heard the approaching truck at the same time and walked toward it. Jorge was driving, with Pilar and Anna next to him, while Mark was precariously perched on the back with the supplies.

Mark jumped down and hugged his sister. "Glad to see you're both all right," he said with a smile as he reached around her to shake Matteo's hand.

Matteo watched as Anna and Pilar alighted. "What are the two of you doing here?"

Pilar brushed the wrinkles out of her fashionable pants. "We thought maybe we could be of some help."

Anna looked right at Christa, but said nothing. She didn't have to. Her message was more than clear. She wanted Christa to stay away from her fiancé.

"Where's the earth-moving equipment we asked for?" Matteo questioned.

"Most of it's on another truck that went on to the valley, and a few pieces are going to be flown in from São Paolo by helicopter," Mark explained.

"Today?"

"That's what we were told. Personally I'll believe it when I see it."

"That's how I feel about most things these days," Matteo told him.

"Was anyone hurt in the flood?" Mark asked.

Matteo looked at Christa, and the same cold fear he felt every time he thought about seeing her hair floating in that water washed over him now. "Your sister nearly drowned."

"What?"

"She was under the water, unconscious, when I found her."

"My god."

"I think those were my exact words."

Jorge moved away from the others and stood next to Christa. "How are things?"

"Fine."

"That's a noncommittal answer if ever there was one."

Suddenly Christa touched Jorge's arm. "Would you help me do something?"

"Of course. What?"

"I want you to help me get out of Brazil without anyone knowing it until after it happens."

"But why?"

"Because I don't want to play this game any longer. I have to get away."

"But what about the wedding? You're Pilar's maid of honor."

"She'll have time to find a new one."

"You're not that easily replaced, you know," Jorge told her as he squeezed her shoulders.

She looked at him with a half smile. "You know, Jorge, I like you very much. It's a shame the two of us didn't meet each other before we met Anna and Matteo."

"I couldn't have said it better myself."

"So, are you going to help me or not?"

"I will. When do you want to go?"

"I'd like to help out here first, but as soon as we're done, I want out."

Jorge nodded. "Very well. I'll see what I can do. Is there anywhere in particular you want to go?"

"To Washington, so I can get a new assignment and clear out my apartment."

"You're going to move?"

"I'm going to start completely over. New city, new apartment, new friends."

"New brother?"

She just smiled. "You're very droll today. I'm just not going to get in touch with Mark and Pilar for a time."

"They'll be hurt."

"Perhaps. For a while. But they'll get over it."

"Christa..."

She sighed. "Look, Jorge, Matteo and I are just torturing each other. We can't help it. It's the nature of what's between us. The best thing I can do for everyone concerned is to put some distance between Matteo and me. Please don't try to talk me out of it anymore."

Jorge raised his hand in surrender. "I'll mind my own business, but I, for one, am going to see this thing through. Anna is wearing down. We had a wonderful time in São Paolo, and I think she got a glimpse into what life with me might be like."

"I hope so, for your sake."

He looked at her for a quiet moment. "You don't have any faith that it's going to work out at all, do you?"

Christa met his look and then turned her eyes away to watch the people in their tent city, loading into the truck and Jeep. "It's harder to give up than to have hope, you know, because for me at this moment Matteo's lost. He's going to spend his life with another woman. His children will be borne by another woman. He'll grow old with another woman." It was hard for her to swallow. "I can't bear to think of him with Anna."

"But you know that he loves you."

"And you think that makes it easier? Well, it doesn't, believe me."

Jorge put his arm around her shoulders and gave her a gentle squeeze. "I'll make the arrangements."

"Thank you."

Pilar was now on the back of the truck, and she leaned over and called to Christa. "Come on!"

Christa kissed Jorge on the cheek and climbed onto the truck with a few others who could fit among the supplies.

She didn't feel Anna's eyes on her, nor had she felt them on her when she'd been talking to Jorge, but they were there. Anna looked from Christa to Jorge and back again, and her teeth worried her lower lip. She was doing the right thing. She had wanted to be a Damiano ever since she could remember, and this was her chance. It was her only chance. She wasn't worried about Matteo deserting her for Christa. He might want the woman, but he wouldn't run off with her. He just wasn't like that.

So what was she so concerned about?

Her eyes rested on Jorge. She was concerned about herself. Why had he come back into her life now? She didn't want him here, filling her with ideas of what life would be like if she chose him over Matteo. She wanted what Matteo offered. He might not love her now, but he would learn to. It would grow between them.

Her gaze searched out Matteo, and she found him. His eyes were on Christa.

Chapter Ten

Christa walked along the lake that was near her parents' home, picking up a rock every once in a while and throwing it in the water. Since she'd left Brazil six months ago, she'd taken one assignment after the other without once returning to her apartment. Her parents were off heaven knew where, and had been for quite a while, judging from the way the house had been closed up when she'd arrived last night. She felt a little guilty about not calling anyone, but she knew that she'd have to hear about the wedding if she did, and she just wasn't ready for that yet.

She sat on the sand, her skirt hiked above her knees, while the breeze blew her hair back, and watched in absolute stillness as the sun set.

But as she sat there, she became aware that she was being watched. There had been no noise. It was just a feeling she had. And she knew who it was. She turned her head and found herself looking into Matteo's brown eyes. They gazed at each other for a long time, but then she looked away, back at the water. "How did you know I was here?"

"I've had detectives watching your apartment and your parents' house. They called last night and said you were here."

Christa trailed her fingers in the sand. "Go back to Brazil," she said quietly.

"Not without you."

"Please, Matteo, I'm just starting to piece myself back together. I don't want to see you now. I can't."

Matteo knelt in front of her and, with a gentle finger under her chin, raised her eyes to his. "Marry me."

Quick tears sprang to her eyes, but her gaze remained unwavering. "That's cruel."

Matteo slowly shook his head. "Christa, I'm not a cruel man. You know that better than anyone."

"But Anna—"

"Is happily married to the man she loves."

"Jorge?"

"Jorge."

"How did that happen?"

A smile touched his mouth. "You should have been there. You would have enjoyed it. She actually made it down the aisle and was standing there with me, and suddenly she stepped back and said she couldn't go through with it."

Christa was still having trouble absorbing what he was saying. "You're free?"

"On the contrary. There's a woman I hope very much will have me as her husband."

Christa went up on her knees and threw her arms around his neck. "I've missed you so much."

His arms went around her and held her close. "You wouldn't have had to miss me at all if you'd only let someone know where you were."

"I didn't want to be found. I couldn't bear to hear about your marriage."

He nuzzled her ear. "You still haven't said that you'd marry me."

She raised her head and gazed into his eyes with such love that it took his breath away. "You tell me where and when, and I'll be there."

"Here. Now."

"You're kidding."

He took her hand and pulled her to her feet. "Come on."

They went up the bank and across the lawn to his car. "Where are we going?"

"To get married."

"But we can't. We have to plan...there are papers...documents..."

"You're marrying a Damiano. Cutting through red tape is one of the privileges."

"I never could stand people who throw their weight around," she said with a smile in her voice.

He parked in front of a small church and walked around to open her door.

Christa stood on the sidewalk next to him. "What if no one's there."

Matteo kissed the top of her head. "Come on."

When they went in, a priest and two people Christa didn't know were waiting for them. Almost in a dream, Christa heard the words that gave them to each other, and in that same dream, Matteo turned to Christa and kissed her tenderly. "Now," he said softly, "we have a plane to catch."

"A plane? But—"

"No buts."

"But I don't have any clothes."

"I'll buy you new ones." He took her by the hand and pulled her behind him.

"I don't want new ones. And where are we going?"

"You ask too many questions." He closed the car door after her and drove to the airport.

His jet was waiting for them. They climbed aboard, and the moment the pilot had closed the door and started the engines, Matteo pulled her into his arms and kissed her until her knees were weak. Then he ran his fingers through her hair and gazed down at her. "I want you to get some sleep."

"I couldn't possibly."

"Try. I want to spend every minute I can with you when we get to Brazil, but in order for me to do that, I have work that needs to be done now."

She kissed his jaw and nibbled his ear. "Now? Why not later?"

"Christa," he said with a groan as he moved her away from him. "Because I want our first night together to be special."

"Just the fact that we're together makes it special."

"I know. But a different kind of special. You'll see what I mean when we get home."

She watched as he went to his desk and started looking at files and making calls. She sat down and tried to read a magazine she found, but she couldn't concentrate. Her eyes kept going to Matteo. And as if he knew when she was looking at him, he would look at her, and a smile of remarkable tenderness would transform his features.

She did manage to sleep a little. She must have, because when she finally opened her eyes, the jet was landing. Matteo kissed her forehead. "Good afternoon."

Christa stretched and wrapped her arms around his neck at the same time. "Good afternoon. Where are we?"

"São Paolo."

She pulled his mouth to hers. Matteo kissed her gently at first, and then more deeply, pulling her body against his.

The pilot cleared his throat behind them.

Matteo raised his head as the grooves in his cheeks deepened. "Have patience. We still have another flight."

They boarded the helicopter and it flew them to the ranch, but instead of taking them to the villa, it flew right past it. Christa looked out the window. "Where are we going?"

"To my grandmother's house. It's finished."

"But Mark and Pilar—"

"Are at the villa. Pilar never wanted the house. She wanted to redo it for us. That's why she had you making the sketches.

"Christa?" he asked when she didn't say anything.

"I loved that house from the moment I saw it. I can't believe she did that for us."

The helicopter landed, and then took off as soon as Christa and Matteo were out of the way. She stood on the bottom step of the porch and shook her head. Flowers had been planted. Wild vines had been clipped and tamed. The porch had been fixed, and the swing had been painted and oiled.

Matteo picked Christa up in his arms and carried her inside, straight up the stairs to the bedroom.

"Don't I get to see the rest of the house?"

"It may be days before you see anything outside of this room." He looked into her eyes and shook his head. "I still can't believe that you're mine. No one can pull us apart anymore." He set her on her feet and cupped her lovely face in his hands, kissing her tenderly, gently at first, then more deeply. He pulled her body close to his, and Christa felt his desire.

Suddenly Matteo wrapped his arms around her and held her tightly.

"What's wrong?" Christa whispered.

He shook his head. "I love you so much that there are times when it overwhelms me. I feel as though I've been given this wonderful gift in you, and I don't ever want to do anything to hurt you, or make you unhappy."

"The only thing you could ever do to hurt me would be to stop loving me. I don't think I could bear that."

His mouth found hers again, and the two of them slowly sank onto the bed. Their clothes fell piece by piece to the floor as they explored every inch of each other's bodies with a slow deliberateness that left them straining against each other.

Matteo raised himself over Christa and gazed down at her before making her completely his, and he knew he'd been right all those months ago.

With his Christa, it had to be all or nothing. He could never have made love to her like this and then let her go. Never.

He tenderly kissed her and pushed her damp hair away from her face. "I love you."

And Christa knew that she would always love Matteo the way she did now. Completely, unswervingly, passionately. They were meant to be.

Silhouette Intimate Moments

MARCH MADNESS!

Get Intimate with Four Very Special Authors

Silhouette Intimate Moments has chosen March as the month to launch the careers of three new authors—Marilyn Pappano, Paula Detmer Riggs and Sibylle Garrett—and to welcome top-selling historical romance author Nancy Morse to the world of contemporary romance.

For years Silhouette Intimate Moments has brought you the biggest names in romance. Join us now and let four exciting new talents take you from the desert of New Mexico to the backlots of Hollywood, from an Indian reservation in South Dakota to the Khyber Pass of Afghanistan.

Coming in March from Silhouette Intimate Moments:

SACRED PLACES: Nancy Morse
WITHIN REACH: Marilyn Pappano
BEAUTIFUL DREAMER: Paula Detmer Riggs
SEPTEMBER RAINBOW: Sibylle Garrett

Silhouette Intimate Moments, this month and every month.
Available wherever paperback books are sold.

IM-MM

ATTRACTIVE, SPACE SAVING BOOK RACK

Display your most prized novels on this handsome and sturdy book rack. The hand-rubbed walnut finish will blend into your library decor with quiet elegance, providing a practical organizer for your favorite hard-or soft-covered books.

Only $9.95

Approximately 16" x 8" when assembled

Assembles in seconds!

To order, rush your name, address and zip code, along with a check or money order for $10.70* ($9.95 plus 75¢ postage and handling) payable to *Silhouette Books*.

Silhouette Books
Book Rack Offer
901 Fuhrmann Blvd.
P.O. Box 1325
Buffalo, NY 14269-1325

Offer not available in Canada.

BKR-2R

*New York residents add appropriate sales tax.

AT LAST YOU CAN FIND
TRUE ROMANCE ON TELEVISION!

PRESENTING THE SHOWTIME●

S E R I E S

Full-scale romance movies, taken from your favorite romance novels. Beautifully photographed on location, it's romance the way you've always dreamed. Exclusively on Showtime cable TV!

ROMANCE ON SHOWTIME
COMING ATTRACTIONS:
CLOUD WALTZING. Based on the Tory Cates novel, starring Kathleen Beller.

ONLY ON SHOWTIME
This winter, look for an Exclusives Explosion on Showtime!
- Exclusive Movies—Down And Out In Beverly Hills, Gung Ho, Fool For Love.
- Exclusive Music Events—Motown On Showtime.
- Exclusive Comedy Series—Brothers, It's Garry Shandling's Show and, of course . . .

ROMANCE ON SHOWTIME—THE ONLY
PLACE ON TV TO FIND TRUE ROMANCE!

SMVA-1

CALL YOUR CABLE COMPANY TODAY TO ORDER SHOWTIME